"I'm not used to anything so soft...."

Kirk's tone reflected the desire in his eyes as he drew Beth into his arms and ran his hand over her robe. "Is your skin as soft as this?"

"Touch me and see," she invited, welcoming his kisses and the feel of his hands, now sliding pink satin off her shoulders.

His lips trailed over her breasts like a brush of fire, and without lifting his head, he murmured, "Ummm ... yes, even softer...."

He continued to explore her mysteries until Beth could stay still no longer. Reaching down, she laced her fingers through his thick hair, then sought his solid shoulders, the dark curls on his chest.... A trembling sigh overtook her and her heartbeat thundered in her ears.

"Tell me what you like, Beth," Kirk urged.

The warmth of his breath sent shivers to her very core, and she breathed, "Everything about you...."

Regan Forest grew up in the Nebraska sandhills, so the setting for *A Wanted Man* is close to her heart. She returned home to research this book, interviewing rodeo cowboys, hanging out at the sales barn and calling up her memories of a Western way of life very different from the one she now leads. At home in Arizona, Regan combines the tasks of raising three children, teaching writing part-time and, of course, crafting blockbuster romances for Harlequin.

Books by Regan Forest

HARLEQUIN TEMPTATION

HARLEQUIN INTRIGUE

A Wanted Man

REGAN FOREST

Harlequin Books

TORONTO • NEW YORK • LONDON
AMSTERDAM • PARIS • SYDNEY • HAMBURG
STOCKHOLM • ATHENS • TOKYO • MILAN

For Beth,
a very special friend.

Published October 1987

ISBN 0-373-25276-5

1

WEAK RAYS OF SUN filtered through the high, barred windows of the Thistle County sheriff's office. Rancid cigar smoke hung in brooding clouds on the pale light, nearly choking the young woman who stood over the sheriff's desk watching him make notes. With a stub of pencil almost swallowed by his large, freckled hand, Ollie Arnold was writing so slowly that she wanted to grab the pencil away from him and fill out the report herself.

"Rocking...T...brand," the sheriff muttered as he formed each word on paper. "You're sure the brand was originally a rocking T, Beth?"

"Of course I'm sure." Sara Beth Connor waved the foul-smelling smoke away from her face and impatiently scraped the heel of her boot against the worn hardwood floor.

Sudden activity outside the open door of the office drew her attention to the outer room. Two uniformed deputies were bringing in a prisoner, and Beth straightened, her stare frozen with curiosity. To witness an arrest in the town of Prairie Hills was unusual enough; the sight of the man—this prisoner—was astounding. Dark, disheveled hair fell over his forehead, and a blue stubble of beard shadowed his face. A face so handsome that Beth drew back and blinked, as though she'd just looked into blinding sunlight.

Almost immediately she was regarding him again, though. When he was led to the main desk for the booking procedure, his back was to her. His hands were cuffed behind him, and she could see the muscles in his shoulders move with agitation against the discomfort of the restraints.

"Rocking T . . ." the sheriff read from his notes, "changed to a closed . . . V . . . mill tail . . . is that right?"

"Yes," Beth answered, no longer intent on the painfully slow process of Ollie's writing.

Light reflected coldly from the steel handcuffs. The prisoner was protesting with his shoulders but not with his wrists; his hands were motionless. His jaw muscles were clenched in a hard knot, another sign of protest to his hapless predicament. She thought how uncomfortable he must be, having his hands forced back and held. Was he so dangerous they couldn't release his hands? Dressed like a typical cowboy in tight, faded jeans, a short-sleeved blue shirt and boots, he didn't look the part of a dangerous criminal. What had this cowboy done?

The sheriff put down his pencil and pushed back a shock of gray hair as he raised his head. "What's going on out there?"

Without waiting for an answer he rose and went to the door, puffing hard on his cigar as he surveyed the booking in progress. A uniformed officer at the desk immediately summoned him.

"Be there in a minute," the sheriff answered with a wave of his cigar. "Soon as me and the brand inspector finish up in here."

He closed the door, and the sound of voices outside disappeared, along with the sight of tanned, masculine hands in manacles. She'd never seen anyone handcuffed before, except in movies. In real life, it seemed a cold and humiliating act. For her, it was unnerving; it wouldn't be easy to forget.

"Never rains but it pours, confound it," Ollie muttered, back to shuffling through papers on his cluttered desk. "Everything going on at once. These drifters is getting common as ticks on a dog anymore. Thieves, all of them. Them and the rustlers combined is gonna cause me an ulcer, surprised if it don't. Now, where the devil were we?"

Beth rolled up the sleeves of her plaid cotton shirt and approached the desk again to have a look at the report.

"Ollie, the Pitman ranch uses the rocking T brand. They're a hundred miles from here, which means this rustling operation is expanding. Something's got to be done."

"We're working on it. Now, you say the sellers that brung in these twelve head today bought 'em eight weeks ago. Where?"

"A private sale in Antelope County. The bills of sale looked in order, but the brand inspector's signature must be forged."

"Yeah. Has to be. Herefords again?"

She nodded. "This is the fourth time in six months I've found altered brands! But I haven't found a fraction of the missing stock from this valley. Most of the rustled animals are being sold elsewhere. If they're getting through smaller auctions or private sales around this part of Nebraska, then some are being passed off as cattle inspected by *me*."

Beth waved at the smoke again. "It's out of hand, Ollie. I've got too wide a territory to cover and I can't begin to try to keep ahead of this. It's impossible. If cattle and horses are being rustled as close to the Colorado border as the Pitman ranch, then we can bet they're being sold in Colorado."

"Yep. And Wyoming." The sheriff rearranged some scribbled reports that Beth was unable to read upside down. "I ain't been sitting warming my backside," he mumbled around his cigar. "I been investigating this thing. At first I thought the cattle thefts and the horse thefts were separate, but since the theft locations correlate, I figure now all the rustling is done by the same bunch. And they're clever. They ain't no amateurs. They've hit every blessed ranch in this valley. You lost some livestock yourself, I recall." The sheriff scratched his head, diligently writing again, the wet, chewed stub of a smoking cigar still in his mouth.

"Ollie, if you don't put that cigar out, I'm going to choke to death! Yes, I've had a prize Hereford bull and a golden palomino stolen. My stepbrother lost twelve head of Herefords from the same pasture. Jed Wilcox lost so much stock when he was sick last winter he's filing for bankruptcy. It makes me furious! We've all, all of us, really had it with these thefts! Don't you have *any* leads?"

Beth cringed watching Sheriff Arnold crush out the cigar stub until it was no more than a half-charred pile of tobacco, inflicting on the thing—for her benefit, no doubt—far more mutilation than was necessary. Finally, he replied, "I'm convinced them rustlers is operating out of Prairie Hills Valley."

Beth paled and took a step back from the desk. Her chestnut hair fell loosely over her shoulders as she gazed at him in anguish. "If that's true, then they're people we know! People stealing from their neighbors!"

"Yep, it looks that way. I got an investigation going, promise you that."

In need of fresh air, Beth started toward the door. "We have to alert buyers about forged papers—tell them what to look for. I'm wondering if some cattle I've inspected at private sales could have been substituted for others at the last minute."

"Maybe. But all them unbranded calves we ain't got no way to check on, since papers can be forged. For every branded critter, they've stole twenty unbranded. All you can do is keep your eye out for anything that don't look quite on the up-and-up. You got good instincts, Beth."

"I thought I did. I still do. I don't think any of the unbranded calves are coming through here."

"Like I said, this bunch is smart. They know you, too. But they're getting awful ambitious. They'll slip up." He rose. "You take care now. Give my best to your stepbrother. I ain't seen Theo in weeks."

The outer area was quiet now, and empty except for two deputies sitting at their desks. Beth assumed their prisoner had been taken through the tall double doors at the back, where a stairway led up to the jail cells.

Slipping the strap of her leather handbag over her shoulder, she hurried down the steps of the building— a slim figure in jeans, her hair loose and flying, her boot heels clicking against the concrete.

Huge old oak and elm trees shadowed the sidewalks along Third Street, shadows just beginning to slant from the west. Five-o'clock traffic was light today, even for a sale day. Promise of a long, balmy evening was in the summer air.

Inside her pickup truck, the warmth of the sun was welcome; it took away the chill she'd begun to feel inside that awful old building. Fumbling for her keys, Beth paused to gaze up at the barred windows on the second floor. She remembered looking up at those same windows when she was a child, both tantalized and aghast to think there were real criminals behind the bars. She'd pictured jail cells as dark and cold and dirty when she was a kid, and she pictured them that way still.

It dawned on her that today was the first time she'd ever visualized a person inside one of those cells—and that person didn't fit her idea of how a criminal should look. Once again she wondered what the cowboy had done to get himself arrested. A drifter wouldn't have been handcuffed unless he was guilty of a pretty serious crime.

THE FOLLOWING SATURDAY AFTERNOON Beth rode her American albino gelding, White Cloud, into the hills— vast prairie hills that rolled out to the horizon. The

Circle C Ranch, all four-thousand acres of it, was hers. She was born here, and her father and grandfather before her. Her great-grandfather, Everett Charles Connor, had pioneered this grazing land more than a hundred years before. The land was part of her, as flesh and blood were part of her. The prairie sandhills were her home—her world.

The day was hot with only a small breeze blowing through tall grass. High, white clouds against blue sky. Lazy hum of insects. Distant cry of a curlew. And the soft rhythm of White Cloud's hooves upon the sandy earth.

She rode past scattered cattle, her stepbrother's cattle, trying to take a random count. It was from this pasture that their livestock had been stolen some months earlier, but she didn't think any cattle were missing now. The herd looked to be intact.

In the distance loomed the high, dark frame of a windmill against the blue sky. At its base, by the round water tank, were the silhouettes of two horses. Beth straightened in the saddle, instantly alert. They kept no horses in this pasture now; something wasn't right. Shading her eyes from the bright sun and squinting as she rode closer, she saw that only one of the horses was saddled, but both appeared to be tethered to a windmill strut.

At still closer range she recognized the sorrel and the Appaloosa as horses belonging to her neighbor, Tom Neilson. Whoever had tethered the animals, Beth deduced, must be swimming in the water tank, a popular respite from the heat of a summer afternoon. But why would anyone be riding Neilson's horses onto her land?

Her body turned cold. Why indeed, unless the horses were being stolen. So this was how they did it! Brazenly *riding* the horses out of the pastures in broad daylight. The rustlers took cattle in a large flatbed truck loaded with hay; this much the sheriff knew. But horses had disappeared one or two at a time. Ridden out, like this!

Heart pounding, she slowed and approached with caution. Her horse's hooves were almost soundless in the thick grass. The singing of insects seemed suddenly softer, so that she was aware of every swish of grass against Cloud's fetlocks, every sigh of his breath and every tiny squeak of the saddle leather.

Red fabric caught her eye first. A shirt hung limply over the bottom support of the windmill, and with the shirt, a pair of faded jeans. Then she saw a man lying naked in the sun.

He was stretched out on his back on a board that covered one side of the stock tank, one arm over his eyes to shield them from the sun's glare. Obviously he was drying off after a swim in the tank and had fallen asleep. He had to be asleep, Beth decided, because he lay so still.

Relief prevailed over the initial shock of encountering a naked horse thief because, for the moment, he posed no danger to her. Unmounted, barefoot and unarmed, he was at a complete disadvantage. Beth's courage lay in the fact that she was on horseback. For some moments she watched him, frantically calculating a course of action. A horse thief caught in the act would be extremely dangerous, yet discovering him like this was an incredible stroke of luck. It was imperative that she get a look at his face so she could identify him.

Her mind whirled around determination and panic . . . and fear. If she could get close enough without waking him, she could free the horses. It would be easier to sneak in on foot but too risky. She'd have to try it mounted. Freeing the horses would strand him here in the hills, meaning a search party could catch up with him easily.

Anger began to dominate fear as Beth recalled the trauma she'd suffered when her palomino, Party Girl, had disappeared two months ago. This had to be the same thief! She vowed to get a look at his face, but that would come later, after she'd made sure he couldn't catch up with her.

White Cloud had a quiet step; for this she was grateful. The other two horses stood quietly, swishing flies with their tails, while she rode in closer. Unfortunately, both the rope that held the Appaloosa and the reins of the sorrel were knotted on the lowest cross strut, almost too low for her to get at while on horseback. She was leaning down over Cloud's stout shoulder, struggling with the knot in the reins, when her movements roused the sleeping man. He woke with a start.

Beth's heart lurched. The still air reverberated with his shout.

"Hey!" He sat straight up. "What the hell do you think you're doing?"

Beth's fingers froze on the knot. She stared in disbelief. This was the same man she'd seen being booked into prison three days ago! The man Ollie Arnold had called a drifter, a thief. He must have been freed on bond, but already he was back to crime. A shiver of fear went through her. She *had* to get the reins untied and set the saddled horse free before he had a chance to stop her.

Perspiration popped out on her forehead; her armpits were damp. Fear of the man numbed her fingers. If she didn't release these horses before he got to her, he might be able to catch her. She knew Tom Neilson's sorrel; a purebred quarter horse, he could outsprint a motorcycle. White Cloud, with his Arabian blood, could outrun the sorrel eventually, provided they weren't overtaken in the first quarter mile. But they would be, if the man decided to leap on and ride naked. Neilson's horse could reach his top speed in two leaps.

The man shouted, "Are you crazy?"

She didn't look up, but his voice was no closer than before. He was still sitting on the board.

The knot gave. She held the reins of the sorrel in her hand. To her surprise, the would-be thief wasn't coming after her. He had slid back into the water, perhaps for modesty's sake, and was shouting curses at her, protesting violently.

"These are Neilson's horses," Beth said, grunting as she leaned over to work at the knot of the rope that held the Appaloosa. "This time you've been caught."

"Lady, you *are* crazy! What are you doing with those horses?"

"I'm going to return them, of course."

"And leave me out here on foot?"

Cloud, stung by a green-headed horsefly, jerked back unexpectedly, startling the other two horses Beth held in tow. Disbelieving anger brutally marred the man's face. What was she waiting for, she asked herself, now that the horses were free? She could leave, lead them back. But something about his voice tempored the spontaneity of her master scheme.

She said, "It's what you deserve. It's better than you deserve."

"Deserve for what? You act like I'm stealing these horses!"

"Aren't you?"

A curse burst from him on an exhaling breath. "I'm working for Tom Neilson."

"Yes . . . I can see you're working." It was as useless to try not to stare at this man now as it had been the last time she'd seen him, at the jail. He stood in the stock tank with the murky water reaching him at midbelly. Deeply tanned and heavily muscled, he was disturbingly handsome. His dark hair, still damp from swimming, curled over his forehead, and even from this distance Beth could tell that his eyes were light blue, almost silver.

"I've been mending fences since sunup. Hell, it's hot out here!"

When he moved, the water rippled around his body and caught the rays of the sun. The dimples of water sparkled. Above them the windmill creaked—a sweet, melancholy summer song. The shadow of the lazily turning blades on the white sand between them was mesmerizing. Their voices carried free on the wind. The horses, bothered by flies, moved restlessly against their restraints.

"You're not on Neilson's land," she said.

"Whose land is it, yours?"

"That's right."

His eyes narrowed. "You got something against a guy cooling off in your horse tank?"

"Of course not. Not usually. Only when it's a horse thief."

Beth was glad she couldn't read lips. No sound came from his, but she could feel the chill of the oath he muttered. Although frightened of him, she felt safe as long as he remained in the tank. If he started out of there, she'd bolt with Tom's horses. With this advantage, she began to calm herself and get control of her trembling. The hundred-in-one chance that she was wrong held in abeyance any action as drastic as leaving him there. It was the indignation in his voice that stalled her.

"I'm not a horse thief and I don't take to being called one! Nor would I take sweetly to being stranded in the hills because of a hysterical woman. I'm warning you not to ride off with that sorrel!"

"Warning me? I don't think you can stop me."

The cowboy's fingers brushed through his hair in a gesture of frustration. His scowl was frightening. "Look, Miss Who-the-hell-ever-you-are, I told you I've been fixing fences and I came through the wire gate back there to get a drink and cool off in the tank. I roped the Appaloosa because she has a cut that needs attention, and I'm getting damned tired of having to stand in the water because I can't reach my pants."

There was a ring of truth beneath the anger in his voice. It was believable that he'd take time out for a swim in the tank. Beth herself often did the same thing on hot summer days, in the privacy of the vast and empty hills.

She slacked the rope and looked over the Appaloosa mare. "Where is she cut?"

"Her off foreleg. I'm surprised you didn't see it."

Beth swung to the right side. He was telling the truth. The cut, probably from barbed wire, needed treatment. It was unlikely a thief would choose an injured horse to steal. She noted, too, that the saddle on the sorrel gelding belonged to Tom Neilson. A local saddle maker made all of Tom's; they were easy to identify.

Still, this man was a criminal. To give him Tom's horse was risky.

"Look," he conceded, "I heard some horses were stolen from these pastures, but I had nothing to do with it. Ride back to Neilson's with me if you don't believe I'm working there. If you leave me stranded up here you'll have to answer to my boss."

Oddly, the anger in his voice kept subsiding and then returning. Beth got the feeling that his indignation at being thought a horse thief was far from genuine, as if he was used to being accused of wrongdoing. It seemed all that really bothered him was having to walk miles on a hot day. Maybe he *was* only a drifter, maybe a petty thief who had been released to Tom Neilson's custody while he waited for his day in court. It was done sometimes when ranchers needed extra help or the jail was full.

The fresh recollection of this man in handcuffs flanked by two sheriff's deputies kept pushing to the forefront of her mind. His silver-blue eyes were impossible to read; they flashed with anger one moment and with something almost like laughter the next, as if he was mocking her.

"All right," Beth agreed, trying to keep her voice steady. "We'll ride back to check out your story with Tom."

She moved up to where his boots lay in the sand at the foot of the windmill, slid out of the saddle just long enough to grab the boots and remounted swiftly.

He watched warily. "Why the devil are you taking my boots?"

"As a precaution. To make sure you don't try anything funny."

His jaw muscles were grinding again. "Like what?"

"Like trying to overpower me."

"Lady, if I wanted to overpower you I'd have done it long before now."

"Would you? In your state of . . . undress?"

For the first time he smiled, but it was a smile without humor. "I'm standing here in the water turning into a prune out of politeness to you, though why I sure don't know. Hell, what's left to hide? How long were you watching me sleep?"

Beth forced herself not to flush; at least, not on the surface so he could see it. Her eyes glanced away, then back. The man had a perfect body, the most perfect she'd ever seen. And he probably knew that. Yes, damn it, he knew a woman couldn't help but admire his body or be stirred by his nakedness whether she wanted to be or not. He was just too good-looking not to know it.

"In that case," she said, ignoring the challenge of his loaded question, "you won't mind getting out of there and getting dressed. That is, if you want to ride back instead of walk."

"Barefoot?" Even from the distance of about twelve feet, Beth could see his eyes spark. "What makes you think I'll stand for that?"

"You have no choice."

"I have several choices, lady. But you're holding more over me than a pair of boots. What I'd like to do right now would get me fired. I can't afford to get Tom Neilson mad enough to fire me."

Of course you can't, Beth thought. *Or you'll end up back in jail.*

He cocked his head toward the windmill shaft. "Do you want my clothes, too?"

She glared at him.

He glared back. "Throw me the clothes, then."

"No. I'm staying on my horse. Get them yourself."

The dark, thick eyebrows arched. Once more she had the feeling he was making lighter of the situation than he tried to let on. Perhaps he was even making fun of her with the strange stare and the hint of teasing that lurked in his voice.

"If that's what it takes to make you happy, ma'am."

The dark, sun-dimpled water churned as he lifted himself out of the tank and back onto the worn, splintery board.

2

WHILE THE COWBOY swung dripping from the board and reached for his clothes, Beth slipped the Appaloosa's rope over the other horse's saddle horn, tied the reins of the sorrel around a windmill strut and backed away. She knew better than to get close enough to hand him the reins.

"You're making a fool of yourself if you think I'm a horse thief," he said with his back to her and one leg in his jeans.

"Maybe. But I have good reasons for my suspicions."

Embarrassed, she averted her eyes, but she was aware that the tight jeans were resisting wet skin. He was having to struggle into them.

He growled, "You can see I'm unarmed."

"I'm not looking at you if that's what you think."

"The hell you're not."

"No, I'm not. Just get on the horse, will you? And take the mare in tow."

"Give me the boots."

"Gladly. At the ranch. I don't trust you."

"You shouldn't, because I can get them away from you."

"You won't, though. Your job, remember?"

His jaw went tight. This was clearly a man more used to giving orders than taking them. "Job or no job, if you were a man you wouldn't get away with this."

Beth forced a smile as she watched him mount and take the mare's rope in hand.

"If you think you can outride me, cowboy, you're mistaken."

He laughed as if the suggestion of her outriding him was a joke. "You're on the wrong horse if you're worried about who can get away from whom."

She blinked. *From whom?* What cowboy ever said "whom"? But the guy knew horses. He knew as well as she did that hers couldn't get away from his on a dash. For a moment, panic returned. She dropped back a safe distance and watched his body move smoothly as he rode in perfect rhythm with the gait of the horse. This was a man who'd spent his life on a horse; she'd bet on it. Maybe he was a drifter, and a lazy one at that— swimming and napping on the job—but he was also a cowboy. He was also a criminal.

He'd made no aggressive move; it looked as though he didn't plan to. Staring at his back and his broad shoulders and heavily muscled arms, she volunteered, "My name's Beth Connor."

"I can't say I'm glad to meet you," he called back.

"What's yours?"

"My name? You wouldn't have ever heard it, ma'am."

They walked the horses at a leisurely pace because the day was hot and getting hotter. Out of the bright blue sky a hawk appeared, soaring directly overhead. The cowboy looked up, shading his eyes to the sun, and reined in his horse to a halt. In fascination, he sat watching the bird. It hung on a current of high wind, almost perfectly still, as if it were weightless, as if, Beth thought, it was some kind of god-like figure looking down to earth. For a full minute the barefoot rider in front of her seemed aware of nothing but the hawk. He sat in solid silence, his gaze on the sky.

He is captivated! Beth thought. Few things on earth were more beautiful than a hawk spreading its wings to conquer the wind, and the wonder of it held this man, made the world stand still for him. And for her. It was a minute of beauty shared—above and apart from the harsh reality of their strained meeting.

The bird circled downward and the man kicked his bare heels into the horse's belly. Riding behind him, Beth could see the sun gleam off his still-wet hair. The guy could bolt, she thought suddenly. Even barefoot and with another horse in tow, he could bolt any minute.

He urged his horse into a canter. She shortened the distance between them, staying close behind, until they reached the buildings of the Neilson ranch.

Tom Neilson was working on the engine of a truck in the yard when the two riders approached. Wiping his greasy hands on a rag, he walked toward them. The cowboy dismounted at once, demanded his boots from Beth, pulled them on quickly while leaning against the shoulder of her horse and stalked off toward the barn leading the two horses, all without saying a word to her or to his boss. Feeling guilty for not believing his story, Beth watched him walk away. The seat of his faded jeans was wet because she hadn't given him a chance to dry off. The boots she'd returned to him were so badly worn she hoped they weren't the only pair he owned but realized they probably were.

Tom Neilson took off his hat and wiped sweat from his forehead with his shirtsleeve.

"Afternoon, Beth. Is there a problem?"

"No problem. Maybe I'm getting too jumpy because of this rustling. When I saw a stranger in the hills with two of your horses, I became suspicious and wasn't sure he was telling the truth when he said he worked for you. It looks like I was wrong."

Tom looked toward the closed barn door. "The guy's a drifter, Beth. Arrested a few days ago for possession of stolen property. I was shorthanded, and Ollie thought it was safe enough to let him work here until his trial comes up. I been keeping an eye on him and no problems so far." Tom Neilson shrugged. "He's a good worker when he decides to work, and he's so anxious to stay out of a jail cell, he's cooperative. He figures I might help him out with the judge later on. I just might if he don't give me no trouble."

Beth explained, "I happened to be at Ollie's office the day this man was arrested. That's why I was hesitant to believe his claim that he worked for you."

Tom lazily patted the neck of Beth's horse and gazed with interest at its blue eyes. Beth was used to people looking at Cloud's eyes; true albinos had pink, not blue, eyes. Cloud, however, was an American albino descended from an Arabian circus horse. Members of his breed had a clear white color, but their eyes were dark.

"How'd you get that cowboy's boots?" Tom asked with a grin.

"He had them off when I came upon him . . . at the windmill." This was all the explaining she intended to do. Beth smiled and turned the reins. "I've got to get home, Tom. Give my best to Sally, won't you?"

While she rode the two miles to the Circle C, Beth's thoughts tortured her with inconsistencies. Why, she asked herself time and again, did the best-looking man she'd seen in years, maybe in her life, have to be a bum? A criminal, just a drifter? She felt uneasy about him, about what had happened in the hills. How smart had it been to make a man like this angry with her? There was a darkness about him that made her shudder; she knew he was telling the truth when he said no man could have gotten away with what she had today. Yet a small glimmer of civility was there, too—civility that had conveyed a message to her female intuition. He wouldn't get rough with a woman.

She'd taken a chance, though, she realized in retrospect, recalling the cold anger in his blue eyes. If he'd wanted to get away from her or hurt her, he could have. Beth tried to shake off the effects of the drifter, tried to think of something else, anything else. But the day's charged moments wouldn't leave her—especially the vision of him lying naked in the sun. Never in her life had she seen so beautiful a man.

EVERY THIRD SUNDAY during the summer months a rodeo was held near the small town of Whiting, fifteen miles north of Prairie Hills. There was no proper rodeo arena here in the heart of the hill land, but a crude facsimile had been improvised years ago. An area of flat ground was fenced, and bucking chutes and a makeshift announcer's stand constructed. Every spring people talked about repainting the wooden chutes, but somehow it never got done, so there were only chips left of the original white paint.

Spectators parked their cars and pickup trucks along the barbed-wire fence and sat on top of the vehicles. Colas, beer and sandwiches in hand, they watched local cowboys compete with each other in the skills by which they made their living.

This summer there was a certain unease within the gathering that had never been there before, brought on by the rustling in the hill pastures and Sheriff Arnold's public suspicions that the thieves were not outsiders. Yet no man suspected his own neighbors or his own hired cowhands, so eventually the crowd got caught up in the spirit of the rodeo.

Beth often worked as a rodeo pickup rider—one of two riders on horseback whose job it was to flank a bucking horse on each side to help a contestant off in case of any difficulty. It wasn't generally considered a woman's job, because masculine strength was sometimes required to grab on to the rider and pull him off. But Beth's riding skills and the dexterity of her blood-bay quarter horse, Pilgrim, made her valuable as a pickup as long as the partner she worked with could supply the power needed in certain kinds of emergencies. Al Duffy, the young cowboy who was riding as her partner today, had the strength of two men.

Halfway into the bareback-bronc-riding event, the loudspeaker boomed out a name Beth had never heard— Kirk Hawthorne. It was unusual at the Whiting rodeo for any but local cowboys to participate, so a small rush of curious comments rumbled through the crowd. Seconds after the rider was out of the chute, Beth recognized him as the drifter—the cowboy she had met at the windmill.

He rode to the eight-second bell easily enough, but the buckskin he had drawn was a "spinner," whirling wildly in one direction, then suddenly in the other, making it impossible for the rider to get off. Beth recognized the horse. It had been used in the last rodeo and had done the same thing, but not with the frenzy it was spinning today. Several attempts to get near the bucking bronc failed.

Kirk Hawthorne had no trouble staying on the horse; his problem was getting off without being hurt. Beth and Al Duffy moved in again, trying to reach him. The bucking horse continued to whirl sideways, oblivious to their interference and clearly oblivious to the barrier of the fence, as well. Hawthorne jerked his left leg forward, lifting it as high as the horse's neck to keep it from being crushed against the front of a pickup truck.

Beth was working frantically trying to get between the buckskin and the fence. It took her several precious seconds to determine in what pattern, if any, the horse was spinning. Al used those seconds to try to get next to the rider; his attempts failed. Now Beth watched for the right opportunity to move in on her side, when the horse was on the crest of the arc of its spin. She was able to get close enough for the rider to grab her saddle horn and pull himself off.

She glimpsed strong, tanned hands clutching the horn of her saddle and felt the press of his body against her thigh as he hung on the side of her horse with his knees drawn up. When Beth had pulled far enough away from the bronc he let go. His boots scraping the ground raised a small cloud of gray dust.

With perspiration staining his shirt and curling his dark hair, the cowboy looked up at Beth with an expression of surprise that told her he realized only now who his pickup rider was. His light eyes held hers for several seconds more, and in those seconds Beth felt her knees grow weak.

It wasn't anger in his eyes this time, but something far different, which she could feel more than see. Reflection of her as a woman was in his eyes, and sparks of pleasure in what he saw. The moment seemed to halt the movement of time, like yesterday's moment of watching a hawk in the sky. She breathed in the dusty aroma of the ring, felt the breeze blowing her hair against her cheek and her horse moving restlessly under her, all in the still-life moment of his stare. His eyes mesmerized her. Thank heavens, she thought, she hadn't been this close to him yesterday, except when he'd taken his boots from her. He'd barely glanced at her then, though, nor she at him.

This time was different; he was in her debt. The bucking horse had been spinning dangerously close to the trucks again when she'd rescued him.

The cowboy blinked and gave her a sign of a job well done. Not a smile, just a quick thumbs-up with a small wave of his arm that meant "Thanks."

For the rest of the afternoon she was conscious of his presence and sometimes of his eyes. And of his impressive skill in the arena. He had an entry in saddle-bronc riding and steer wrestling, even calf roping—using Tom

Neilson's sorrel quarter horse. This man was no stranger to a rodeo. He was good, almost too good for these local cowboys to compete with.

Beth noticed him once leaning against the fence of the bull pen, drinking a cola and looking over the half-dozen bulls. Most of them were at least part Brahma, easily recognized by their humped shoulders and almond-shaped eyes. Beth admired the incredible beauty of the Brahmas, but these! Some of these crossbred bulls looked more mean than beautiful. Kirk Hawthorne was picking out one he had drawn, she figured, to see what sort of look was in its eyes.

For the bull-riding contest, the arena was cleared of all horses and people, except for the rodeo "clown" and his large protective barrel. Dressed in red long johns, it was the clown's job to distract the bull from contestants, allowing them to get out of the arena safely after the ride. The bulls were dangerously unpredictable. Too often they charged a rider once his feet were on the ground, and a successful charge from an animal this big and this mean could be fatal. Why any man would want to ride the ornery creatures Beth had never been able to fathom. She knew it had something to do with the challenge of pitting one man's courage and skill against another—something that seemed extremely important to men. And often fascinating—if not very sensible— to women.

She found herself fascinated now, as always. Having joined her friends she sat on the cab of a pickup parked next to the bucking chutes to watch the bull riding, the last event of the day.

When his turn came, Kirk Hawthorne lowered himself into the narrow chute onto the back of a white Brahma bull. The animal fought so wildly the cowboy had to climb back up and try again. It took three attempts to mount the bull before he succeeded. Each time the other contestants hanging on the chute jumped down to distance themselves from the danger. His competitors cocked their heads, emitting low whistles. This was a new bull to the Whiting rodeo-stock collection, one lent by the Triple Wing Ranch. Not only was he large, he obviously didn't like where he was and didn't intend to be ridden.

Out of an awed hush came Hawthorne's signal that he was ready. "Let 'er go!" he yelled. The chute gates opened and the Brahma lunged into the arena, a monster gone mad.

Kirk managed to stay on until the eight-second bell, the only rider so far that afternoon to do so. There was no question his was the winning ride. He let go of the rope and allowed himself to be thrown off, landing with a thud on his back. The bull turned suddenly toward him, bent on revenge. Kirk scrambled onto his feet and headed for the protection of the barrel. The rodeo clown interceded at once, waving his arms, successfully distracting the huge animal so the cowboy could get out of the arena. After the close call, Kirk appeared to be less concerned with the applause for his superb ride than where the Brahma bull was, behind him.

Beth watched him climb onto the side of the chute just under the announcer's stand while other rodeo contestants congratulated him on the ride. Dust was clinging to the back of his sweat-soaked shirt and his dark hair was in his eyes. She thought what a picture he made in tight jeans and boots and a blue short-sleeved shirt that pulled against bulging muscles. And she knew that every woman in the crowd must be looking at him, thinking the same thing, wondering who he was.

Always after the rodeo a barbecue and barn dance were held at a ranch near the rodeo grounds, a celebration complete with a live western band from Prairie Hills and unlimited free beers for the day's winners.

While she showered and changed clothes at the home of a friend in Whiting, Beth was preoccupied with confusing thoughts of a cowboy who had claimed today's first prizes for bull riding and saddle-bronc riding. The way he had looked at her through the rising dust as his feet touched ground was indelibly imprinted on her mind. His expression had held more than surprise when he'd discovered she was his pickup rider. His face had revealed a man seeing a woman. And the effect had been electrifying. The memory sent a tremble through her.

He would probably show up at the dance—everybody did, Beth thought as she dressed in fresh jeans and a pale-pink shirt. That possibility made her uneasy. Would he be civil to her after the stunt she'd pulled yesterday in the hills? He'd told her she was making a fool of herself, and in retrospect, she certainly had.

It was interesting that Tom had let him use his horse for the roping. Maybe Hawthorne's crime wasn't all that grievous, or else he'd done a good job of getting Tom to like him. In either case, whatever he was accused of stealing clearly wasn't livestock.

At the barbecue she caught sight of him once or twice through the crowd. If he saw her, he gave no sign of it.

At eight o'clock the barn doors were opened wide and the band began to play dance tunes. The building was a large old structure. Having been replaced by a more modern barn for livestock, this one was now used only for storing hay and grain. It's cement floor, strewn lightly with fresh hay, was fine for dancing. The stage for the band was an antique hay wagon, and a make-shift bar had been set up in one corner of the enormous lower room. Above, in the loft, most of the hay bales had been pushed against the walls.

There was no one here Beth didn't know at least by name. While she talked with her friends and danced, she saw Kirk Hawthorne from time to time, but never on the dance floor. The only stranger among them, he was nevertheless mingling easily with people, laughing, probably accepting repeated congratulations on his winning rides. His skill had won him more than money today; it had won him their respect. *He's done rodeos before, and plenty of them,* Beth thought for the dozenth time. *He rides like a pro.* It would be interesting to know how he'd come up with the entry fees.

At first, Beth told herself she was relieved that he hadn't spoken to her, but gradually she came to admit the relief was being drowned in disappointment. He probably didn't think she deserved a civil word. Yet her close-held memory of the look in his eyes earlier that day seemed to fall over all other images like the swirls of dust through which she'd seen him and, like dust, cover over whatever lay underneath, whatever had come before.

For her, it was this way. But then, she was the one
who had been wrong yesterday. She was the one who—
Beth winced and colored at the thought of him climb-
ing naked from the tank at her insistence. *If that's what
it takes to make you happy, ma'am,* he had said. The
words smarted. Scalded.

Women were surrounding him tonight; that was no
surprise. Once, when the music was loudest and she
had left the dance floor, Beth saw him standing at the
bar, for the moment alone. He had changed into a clean
white shirt, but his jeans and boots were still streaked
with rodeo dust. He was drinking from a bottle of beer
and watching the band.

Although it was too late to change yesterday, Beth
didn't want this man as an enemy. With palms sweat-
ing and knees feeling a little uncertain, she summoned
the courage to approach him.

"I'd like to apologize for yesterday. I overreacted. I'd
lost a horse myself from that pasture, and you
were . . . and I—"

"Forget it," he interrupted in a mild voice. "I owe you
for today, so we're even."

Beth looked not at him but at the band. The lead
guitarist was gyrating all over the little stage. "Not
really. Any pickup would have done the same."

"I don't think so. I was about to get my leg broken
because the damned horse wouldn't get away from the
fence. The way you came in was real slick. Only a sharp
and experienced pickup could have done it."

"You're experienced in the rodeo arena yourself. That
was clear today."

"Is that a compliment, Miss Connor?"

She nodded. "You remember my name."

"I remember everything."

She flushed and tried to concentrate on the guitar player.

He asked, "Do you?"

"Do I what?"

"Remember everything?"

He was getting even, after all. Beth swallowed and shrugged with pretended innocence and wished she hadn't started a conversation with him at all.

Sounds of country music filled the space between them until he said, "I probably even remember how to dance, though it's been a long while. Are you a good dancer?"

"I . . . guess so."

"Want to?"

She looked at him. He was smiling. "Sure." She smiled back. "Why not?"

He took her cold hand in his warm one and led her to the center of the dance floor, then pulled her gently—surprisingly gently—into his arms.

"We lucked out," he said. "A slow song. Jumping-around songs aren't my thing. Matter of fact, dancing isn't my thing, but once in a long while I get inspired."

"By having a winning day?"

"Nah. By a girl with hair that shines in the sunlight and who rides like she was growed to the saddle."

Her nose wrinkled. "Growed to the saddle?"

"That's an expression my old daddy used to use. Take it as a compliment." He hummed to the music for a time and then said, "I asked about you at the rodeo and was told you own the Circle C Ranch. That's quite a spread of land to be owned by one little bitty gal."

"It was my father's."

She felt his arms tighten around her. His voice softened. "All my father left me was a rusty musket that he swore my great-grandpa once killed ten Indians with. Probably a lie. I come from a long line of liars."

Beth had been held by men before, but not like this. Everything about Kirk Hawthorne—his voice, his eyes, his touch—unnerved her. He held her softly and sensually against his body as they danced, and now so close she could feel his heartbeat.

She tried to discourage the racing of her own heart by reminding herself that the hand holding hers so gently now had not very long ago been shackled by handcuffs. But the mind games she tried to play didn't work. Another picture was too much stronger—his tanned, naked body motionless in sleep....

Oh, yes, I remember, she thought, feeling uncomfortably warm in his arms. *You know damn well I remember!*

3

THEY SAT in the hayloft, dangling their feet over the edge and watching the activity on the dance floor below. The music was softer because the hour was late. Since their first dance, they hadn't parted company. The rest of the evening had been theirs together, on the dance floor mostly, until they'd climbed up to the loft and settled onto loose fresh-smelling hay to talk.

"You don't run your ranch alone, do you?" Kirk asked.

"No. My stepbrother and stepmother manage it with me. Actually, I have far less stock than they do. Theo, my stepbrother, has more time for the ranch than I do."

"Why is that?"

"I have another job. I'm a brand inspector."

That seemed to surprise him. He took a swallow of beer, leaned back on his elbows and looked at her quizzically.

"I learned the job from my dad," she volunteered. "And I've been doing it since long before he died."

Kirk fell into a strange silence.

She said, "You haven't talked about yourself. Where are you from?"

"Montana. Right now I'm sort of . . . traveling."

"Looking for permanent work?"

He avoided making direct contact with her eyes. "Nah. I was on the rodeo circuit for a while, quit that when I broke my collarbone and been down on my luck ever since. Guess I'm not good at much of anything else. I'm sure no good at staying put. I like to keep on the move."

Or do you mean on the run? she thought. If he was a rodeo professional, which was easy to believe after seeing him perform today, then he had no business riding in their little local rodeo, competing with cowhands who had spent hard-earned wages for entry fees. Not only was it unfair, it was probably illegal if he belonged to the Rodeo Cowboys' Association. And he had to be a member of that organization if he had ever been a pro. Clearly, Kirk Hawthorne was a man of questionable principles. He seemed to have no roots, or he couldn't talk too much about himself because he had tracks to cover.

Nevertheless, he was so likable and so attractive. Everything about him drew out her curiosity and her fascination.

Leaning back on his elbows, tapping time to the music with his fingers, he smiled slowly. "I've made some enemies here tonight. A lot of guys wanted to dance with you and I gave them my one-step-closer-and-you're-dead look."

"I know. I saw you."

"You didn't get mad."

Beth smiled.

"I was waiting for one of them to take me on."

"You were? Which one?"

"Whichever one thinks he has a right to."

"In that case, you were safe."

"Yeah?" Kirk straightened. "You mean you're not..."
He fumbled for a word.

"Not what?"

"Not . . . taken?"

Beth's mischievous smile was her only answer.

"How come you're not? A lady as pretty as you? You
ever been married?"

"No. I was engaged. My fiancé owned an import
business in Omaha. He went to Tokyo on a business trip
and came home three months later with a Japanese
wife."

Kirk blinked. "Whoa, that's slightly rough! And
you're permanently stunned and bitter. Right?"

"Wrong. I really wasn't terribly sure about getting
married anyhow, because I hated to leave the ranch. To
live in a big, bustling, crowded city, I'd have had to give
up an awful lot. Too much, I think." She turned toward him. "What about you? You're not married, are
you?"

"Me? The way I live? Nah."

"Were you ever?"

He paused. "Once. I was on the rodeo circuit then.
It didn't work."

There were inconsistencies about this man, Beth
thought. Certain expressions in his face and in his
speech didn't fit an aimless drifter. And the gentleness
about him came disguised, but not disguised well
enough. She'd sensed that gentleness even at their first
encounter. Kirk Hawthorne confused her, and her own
response to him confused her even more.

Women—the women at the dance—stared at him partly because he was a stranger but mostly because he was so good-looking. Kirk didn't seem to notice; probably he was used to it. But Beth became more and more aware of the stares during the course of the evening. She felt eyes on them now.

"Someone's trying mighty hard to get your attention, Beth," Kirk said, nodding toward the dance floor below them. "I take it you know that guy who's waving up here."

"That's Theo, my stepbrother. It looks like he wants to talk to me." She waved back and got to her feet. "I can't imagine what could be so important it couldn't wait until morning."

"From the anxious expression on his face, I'd guess it's pretty important."

She nodded. "Excuse me, then, Kirk. I suppose I'd better find out."

Other people who were sitting around the loft on bales of hay moved out of the way to allow her to pass across to the ladder.

Theo Lebs waited for his stepsister in a shadow-filled corner. Tall, blond, bearded, he was lighting a cigarette as she approached. He was not smiling. Theo usually smiled; it was his nature. But the look Beth saw in his eyes in the flame of his cigarette lighter was a look of genuine anxiety.

Beth brushed back her shoulder-length hair and narrowed her gaze. "What's the matter, Theo?"

He was leaning against the wall. His voice was gentle, hesitant. "Rumors are spreading all over the dance about that guy you've been with all evening. I hate to be the one to tell you this, Beth, but the guy's a criminal. A thief. He was arrested in Prairie Hills a few days ago. Right now he's out on bail."

She sighed. "I know."

"You *know*?" Her stepbrother acted as if he had just been slapped.

She suddenly realized there were more reasons for the stares than Kirk Hawthorne's handsome face. Rumors were sizzling and bubbling all over this place.

"Did Hawthorne tell you?" Theo asked.

"No. I . . . heard it."

"Then how can you . . . ?" He paused and gazed around the room, his jaw muscles tightening. "Beth, honey, this guy is bad news. It's none of my business, I guess, but I felt I ought to warn you. I thought you didn't know."

"For heaven's sake, Theo, I'm only talking to him."

"And dancing with him, while he acts like no other man in this barn had better come near you if he wants to keep his teeth."

She couldn't help smiling, which made Theo smile, too, and then laugh. Laughing, he insisted, "It's not funny."

"Then why are we laughing?"

"Because . . . because everybody is so horrified at seeing you chum up with this unsavory character. I've been watching them watching you."

She grinned innocently. "And that's funny?"

"Yes, damn it . . . no. No. Hell, I don't see how I can protect your reputation if you won't take my genuine concern seriously."

"My reputation, is it?"

Affectionately he circled his arm around her shoulder and drew on his cigarette. "He's a criminal and a drifter, Beth. That's what they're saying about him."

"What crime do they say he committed?"

"It varies. You know how rumors spread like a prairie fire. I've heard everything from car theft to horse theft to murder."

"*Murder?*"

He shrugged. "Well, I don't believe all of it. I don't think I believe the murder part if he's running around attending barbecues."

"Neither do I." She wrinkled her nose. "He may be unsavory on the inside, but he looks real good on the outside, Theo. And he's rodeo champion of the day."

"And he was quick to pick out the prettiest girl in this room. I'll give him credit for his taste in ladies. Yeah, I'll give him that much, at least. But, honestly, Beth, seriously, the rumors are flying around this place like a flock of moths flying around a lamp. And I'm afraid you're the lamp."

"Does it bother you?"

He cocked his head sideways and studied her. "Not if it doesn't bother you. I'm just playing big brother here. I don't want some bum who won't be truthful about his real identity interfering with my little sister's reputation. If any guy ever tries to hurt you in any way, he'll have to answer to me. I don't care how damn tough he thinks he is."

She smiled. "You're appreciated, Theo. You're acting perfectly paranoid, but I suppose it's because you care, and I love you for it even if you are being ridiculous. This rodeo cowboy has no intention of hurting me. We're just . . . just talking."

"Yeah, I know, but come on, kid, let's go home. Leave the bum where you found him. You know the barrage of rumors is going to get right back to Mother and she'll be horror-struck and think your life is in danger. Or worse, that your status as a single lady is in danger."

Beth laughed. "Worse than that. She'll have to face the girls in her Tuesday-afternoon bridge club."

"Yes, she will."

She gazed at him, serious now. "Lila wouldn't like this, would she, Theo? Your mother looks on everything as a personal family matter."

"Well, it is, in a way. What one of us does always affects the others—like in a real family."

"We are real," she said. Theo and his mother did consider the three of them a family. And it was true they were all the family she had. His mother, Lila, had married Beth's father only four years before he died. Theo had been in Australia then. He'd returned two years ago after Lila was widowed, to learn that the Circle C Ranch had been left in its entirety to Beth but with the stipulation that Lila could remain at the ranch for as long as she lived.

Lila and Theo did very well there, with a sizable herd of their own. Beth had been pleased with the arrangement, and she enjoyed them both, and the three of them had gotten along well and smoothly. They'd become a family.

Beth waved his cigarette smoke away from her face and leaned closer to him. She whispered, "The talk about murder is so stupid! Tom Neilson told me Kirk Hawthorne was arrested for theft and released on bail."

"Tom Neilson isn't even here. When did he tell you that?"

"Well . . . earlier. Kirk is working over there at the Neilson ranch while he's waiting trial."

Theo grinned. "You are full of mischief, aren't you, Beth? You knew all along."

"Maybe."

"The next thing you're going to tell me is you like this weird character."

"He's interesting."

"So is a rattlesnake. And just about as deadly, if you want my opinion."

"I don't, especially."

"You got it anyhow." Theo threw down his cigarette and stomped it out with his boot heel. "Come on home with me, honey. Before things get any hotter in this place."

"I'm not slinking out of here like I've done something wrong. I haven't."

"Then do it for my sake. Because if this guy tries to get any chummier with you, I might just have to get chivalrous and gallant. And I'd rather not have to, because from the looks of him, I may not get out of here with all my teeth and hair." Theo cringed. "He has the look of a potential killer."

"Oh, he does not, Theo! I can't believe how you're overreacting."

"Don't I always? I always overreact, you know that. So indulge me. Honor is at stake here."

"Whose?"

"Hell, everybody's. If you ask me, we should slink. I'm trying to help, damn it."

His left eye was squinting as it always did when Theo was genuinely nervous about something. He was pretending to take this lightly, but he was concerned, for her sake. Maybe he had reason to be. Maybe she really had been reckless this evening, consorting with a known criminal.

She turned away from her stepbrother and looked up to the loft. Kirk was no longer sitting there. He didn't seem to be anywhere in the thinning crowd. Somehow she hadn't expected him to leave without saying goodbye to her, after they'd spent so much of the evening together. Perhaps he sensed that her stepbrother wanted to warn her about keeping company with him. Perhaps all the stares hadn't gone unnoticed after all. Or perhaps he was simply tired of the party and wanted to go.

"I'm not leaving without you," Theo was saying, lighting another cigarette. "I want to make sure you get home all right."

Beth sighed deeply, sadness sweeping over her—a sense of loss for the end of a special night. The end of a special something.

"Okay. Let's go, then," she said, taking a firm hold on her stepbrother's arm and ignoring the stares and whispers that followed them out of the barn.

BREAKFAST THE FOLLOWING MORNING was a strain. Beth knew the moment she came downstairs that last night's dance had been the subject under discussion. That meant her stepmother had already been briefed by someone. Theo was right—rumors spread over this valley like a prairie fire whipped by wind.

Beth had heard the phone ring earlier this morning—probably Irma Wampler with the news. Irma had an uncontrollable compulsion to scoop everybody with gossip, and this tale was too hot to keep on hold until after breakfast, when half the town would be up and dialing. Lila Connor, wearing a simple cotton dress with a pink-and-white floral design, was seated in her usual place at the table, pouring coffee from a china pot. Her "Good morning" was uncertain, almost shaky.

"Well," Beth said, handing her empty coffee cup to her stepmother. "I bet you've been talking to Mrs. Wampler this morning, and I bet Irma wasn't discussing her arthritis, for once."

Lila was pale. "Irma was full of the most awful gossip. I was sure it was nothing but lies. But then I asked Theodore if it was true, and he said it was."

Theo was grinning as he buttered his toast. A spray of sunshine from the window sparkled on the silver knife and reflected brightly in the mirrored wall. "So rumbles a scandal across our green and peaceful valley!"

"You seem to be taking this very lightly," Lila said. "Both of you."

Beth helped herself to a cinnamon roll. "It doesn't amount to anything."

"How can you say that? Did you or didn't you spend the entire evening with a convicted criminal?"

"I don't think he's convicted yet."

Lila looked helplessly at her son. "You were there, Theo. Why didn't you protect Beth from this man? Obviously she didn't know what he was."

"Well, I did try, Mother. I was well-intentioned as hell. Now, that's the living truth. And actually, I did rescue her, I think. Didn't I, Beth?"

"Yeah, I think you did," she said sourly.

The older woman looked from one to the other, confusion in her eyes. Beth felt sorry for her. There was no telling what proportions the story had reached before it left the wagging lips of Irma Wampler.

"What did happen last night?" Lila asked softly.

"I danced with this guy and talked to him, not realizing that the whole place was rocking with rumors about him. That's the whole of it, Lila. Really."

"And Theo rescued you? Did he?"

Beth laughed. "I didn't need rescuing. Kirk Hawthorne acted . . . He was very nice."

"And interesting—don't forget interesting," Theo added, chewing while he sliced ham and not looking up from his plate.

"But . . ." Lila began to stammer nervously. "But, Beth, dear, your reputation . . ."

"Good grief, Lila, I can't live my life worrying about what other people think—or say. That's no way to have to live, is it?"

The older woman twisted her wedding band—the one that had not been off her finger since the day Beth's father placed it there, on their wedding day, six years ago this month. "But, dear—a jailbird? A murderer?"

"He's not a murderer," Beth sighed.

"But Irma told me—"

"Oh, come on, Lila. You've never listened to Irma Wampler in your life."

"What could Irma possibly know?" Theo asked mildly, wiping orange juice from his mouth. He was not allowing this emotional matter to interfere with his breakfast, even though the two women had barely eaten at all.

"At the very best, he's a jailbird and a worthless drifter. My point is, it's just not like you, Beth. Why would you do it?"

Beth sipped her black coffee. "I don't know how to answer you, Lila. Maybe I don't know why myself. I do know that Kirk Hawthorne is better-looking than any *honest* man I know. Is that a good reason?"

"Oh, Beth!" Lila looked helplessly at her son once again.

"It's true, Mother," Theo said. "And he can ride bulls like nobody I've ever seen. Hell, from his performance yesterday, I doubt there's anything on four legs the guy can't ride. Quite a figure he is—on or off a bull." He popped a large bite into his mouth and waved his fork. "Actually, I think there were more than a few envious faces behind the whispers last night. If you ask me, that's why the rumors went so wild so fast."

"Why?" Lila asked. "Because this . . . drifter is good-looking? Is that what you're saying, Theo?"

"Yep. I'm saying that. I'm saying there was some plain old jealousy there."

"Jealousy over a *murderer*?"

"He isn't a murderer," Beth repeated patiently. "He's merely a thief."

"Just a simple thief," Theo confirmed.

Lila raised her arms in the air in a gesture of frustration. "You two may not take this seriously, but I must. I'm older. I've seen more. Beth, I pray you're not going to be taken in by this drifter! I know his kind well! They have one dream, all of them. They want to marry money, preferably ranch money. I'll bet a thousand to one that before the dance ever started he already knew you own the Circle C Ranch, and then he asked you right off the bat if you were single."

Beth felt a wave of shame and fear. Lila had always been a good judge of character. But this time Beth wanted desperately for Lila to be wrong. Lila *could* be wrong, even though everything had happened exactly as she'd said!

Get real, Beth scolded herself in a flush of humiliation. What could she expect, anyhow? She knew what Kirk Hawthorne was. Wishing he was something different wouldn't make it so.

4

THUNDER CRACKED LOUDLY OVERHEAD. Lightning lit the night sky in bright flashes as Kirk made his way from the barn to the house, his shoulders hunched against pelting rain, his boots sloshing in deep mud.

In the shelter of the small front porch, he leaned against the building, pulled off the boots and pounded them against the step. The mud stuck stubbornly. Cursing softly, he set the boots on the porch and went inside in stocking feet.

It was a small white frame house with a living room, kitchen and two bedrooms, starkly furnished. The hired man and his wife who had lived there before him had done some painting and left figured curtains made from flour sacks at the windows. The couple had decided suddenly to return to Arkansas in late spring, and Tom Neilson had been left shorthanded in the calving season.

Kirk peeled off his wet clothes and got under a hot shower. His shoulders were aching from an afternoon of digging postholes. This was more work than he'd bargained for, and he intended to complain to Ollie Arnold about it. A deal was a deal, but fourteen-hour days and slogging through mud up to his ankles was too much. If something didn't break soon, his back would. He'd give it another week and then pack it in. The sheriff would have to find somebody else. This slave labor wasn't what he'd been hired for.

He was certain by now that Tom Neilson was honest as they come. Tom himself had lost fifteen head of Herefords to the rustlers in winter and six spring calves. But still, Kirk couldn't risk confiding in Tom about who he really was, even if it would lessen the work load. People didn't keep secrets well; he'd learned that long ago. Trusting anyone could jeopardize his chances of success, especially here in this valley, where neighbors trusted neighbors.

But somewhere the rustlers would slip up. Their operation was getting bigger and their territory broader. They'd have to have more people involved. That was what Ollie Arnold had told the national cattlemen's group who sent a spokesman all the way to Montana to hire a professional to infiltrate the rustling ring.

Kirk had worked undercover before. He was good at it—much better than he was at mending fences and pulling calves and digging holes in the mud. Hell, he thought as he emerged dripping from the shower, danger, even hard labor weren't the part of a lawman's work he hated most—it was the cursed waiting.

The rodeo had worked to draw plenty of attention to him and to his skills. Rumors of his arrest and unsavory reputation must have spread over half the county by now. It was only a gamble that this would bring the snakes crawling out from under the rocks to proposition him, but it was a well-calculated risk. If the ploy was going to work, though, something would have to happen soon.

Kirk dried off and slid into jeans and a sweatshirt. The slapping of rain on the roof muffled the usual creaks and groans of the old house. Thunder rumbled. A scratching came at the door.

Kirk smiled as he walked through the darkened living room, drying his hair with a towel. It would be old Mitzy at the door, one of the ranch's mongrel dogs who had come around to the little house the first night Kirk was there and had slept beside his bed every night since. He'd seen Mitzy in the warm barn an hour ago, stealing food that had been left out for the cats. Kirk was impressed she'd braved a downpour like this for the sake of their friendship. He welcomed the soaked black dog, drying her vigorously with the towel even though muddy paws streaked his clean jeans.

Ten minutes later Kirk was lounging on his bed, strumming his guitar. He was barefoot, and his hair was still damp from the shower. Mitzy was settled happily on the rug. Soft strains of music floated through the noise of the rain and lulled her to contented sleep.

Kirk leaned his head back against the headboard and hummed as he played. Sad songs and love songs kept floating to the edge of his consciousness and spilling out as music. A woman was vibrant and vivid in his thoughts, more so even than she had been yesterday or this morning, after the dance. More so than he wanted. He thought of chestnut hair, how soft it felt against his face when he'd held her, dancing. He thought of hazel eyes and how they'd laughed and how they'd questioned, and how sometimes they'd looked at him so strangely.

Beth thought he was a worthless bum. Worse, she thought he was a thief. But that's what he'd intended for Prairie Hills to believe, wasn't it? Great! Beth thought he was a bum and there was nothing he could do about it.

She'd been pleasant to him last night and fun, but he couldn't expect a woman like her to have much to do with a man she believed was a thief awaiting trial and a jail sentence. The rhythm of raindrops against the window, mixed with the melancholy strains of his guitar, kept the thoughts of her near him. He hadn't counted on this, hadn't counted on meeting Beth.

Pounding on the front door startled him. The dog sat up and gave a sharp bark. Kirk thought that surely Sally Neilson, thoughtful as she was, wouldn't come out in a driving rain to bring him a slice of cake. Often she did bring him hot cocoa and cake or pie on nights when he'd been working late after supper. Sally's cooking was the one good thing about this lousy job. But whoever was banging on the door couldn't be Tom's wife, not tonight.

Kirk lay his guitar on the bed and walked barefoot over the worn carpet, noticing as he turned on the living-room light for the first time tonight that the ceiling was leaking badly in one corner. An overstuffed chair was getting soaked. Quickly he moved the chair out from under the drip and turned on the outside porch light. Mitzy was barking at the door by the time he opened it. In the light from the porch, he could see a green pickup truck parked outside. Strange he hadn't heard it pull up, he thought; the rain didn't seem *that* loud.

A short, balding cowboy removed his Stetson and hesitated at the door. "Does that mean-looking flea-bag bite?"

"Only when she's called a fleabag," Kirk answered.

The man stepped back uncertainly. "What's her name?"

"Killer."

"Nice Killer," the cowboy cooed as he stepped inside, extending his hand, keeping one eye on the dog. "Marty Schock. Remember me?"

All Kirk's instincts as a lawman were alerted at once. This was no social call, not at this hour, in this storm. He smiled, "Sure, I remember you. From the rodeo. You drew the piebald bronc that did a twist sideways every time she came out of a kick."

"Cursed horse. If I'd stayed aboard, though, she'd have got me the bareback purse."

"Yeah, she would have," Kirk agreed, reaching for the screen door that had blown against the side of the house when he opened it. A gust of rain-soaked wind blew in.

"If you'd drawn that pinto instead of the stupid spinner you got, you'd have rode her and won that event, too."

"You think so?"

"Yep. I was watching you all day. You ain't no beginner."

Kirk grinned. "You didn't come out here just to tell me that. Come on inside, if you don't mind kicking off your boots. I hate cleaning mud off the floor."

The ceiling drip was making a puddle. "I've got to get something for that damned leak," Kirk said. "Sit down if you want. I'll be right back."

When he returned from the kitchen with a wide-mouthed pickle jar, his guest was seated in stocking feet on the couch across from the drip, lighting a cigarette and staring back at the dog, who was crouched in the middle of the room glaring at him suspiciously. There were streaks on the man's shoulders from the rain, but he hadn't gotten very wet making the short dash from his truck to the porch.

Kirk patiently centered the jar directly under the leak. He stood, watching the drops plink in. "What's on your mind, Marty?"

"You got any coffee?"

"Yeah, I've got instant."

"I'll take anything that's hot and strong. It's cold in here."

Kirk had no teakettle in the sparsely equipped little kitchen. He set water to boil in a saucepan and returned to the living room.

His unexpected guest, rubbing his hands against the cold, got directly to the point. "I'm told Tom Neilson went your bail and you're up for a robbery trial. That true?"

Kirk rubbed his chin and squinted at the other man. "Who told you that?"

"Hell, there ain't no secrets in Prairie Hills."

Kirk shrugged. "No point in my denying it, then. I can't say there'll be any trial."

"You're pleading guilty, huh? They nailed you solid, huh? How soon's your hearing gonna be?"

"Several weeks is my guess. I know what's going on. Tom Neilson will hang on to me as long as he can because he lost a hired hand. Tom's on the city council.

He'll get my hearing postponed until he's hired some-body else, and that's not likely to be soon because a man would have to be nuts to take this stinking job. It's better than jail is all I can say for it." He squinted again at his guest. "You got some reason for asking?"

Marty Schock sat ankle over knee. The soles of his socks were black. "When I seen you yesterday, I fig-ured you was a rodeo pro. I also figured you was used to being on the move and not real pleased having to stay in one place. Did I get that right?"

"Maybe."

"What'd they nail you for?"

"Theft." Kirk's voice was cold now. He got up to check the water on the stove. "That's all I'm gonna say. It's my business, not yours, even if it is all over the damned valley. Are you just nosy as hell, mister, or did you come here for a reason?"

"Sure I got a reason. Would I half drown myself in this weather to drive ten miles for a cup of instant cof-fee?"

Kirk brought out two steaming mugs.

His guest cupped the mug in his cold hands and sipped gratefully. "Have you thought about jumping bail?"

Kirk sat down across from him. The drip was ping-ing melodically in the pickle jar. The rain began to fall more softly on the roof. The house smelled damp and old.

"I thought about jumping bail. Decided against it. There's already three states I can't set foot in, though good old Sheriff Ollie hasn't found that out. I figure I can win over Tom Neilson and he'll be influential in getting me off light."

"I noted you was roping off Neilson's best horse. Is he paying you anything?"

"Neilson?" Kirk scowled. "Piddling."

"You interested in making some money?"

"Legal or illegal?"

Marty crushed out his cigarette in the ashtray on the wobbly coffee table and finally took his eyes away from the dog. "Illegal."

Kirk paused thoughtfully, rubbing the stubble of beard on his chin. "No. I got problems enough as it is."

"Hell, it's good money, easy work. Real easy work for a man like you. Just requires a few hours of your time."

"What do you mean, a man like me?"

"You been on the circuit, ain't you?"

"What if I have?"

"What was your specialty? Bulls?"

"And saddle broncs. But I'll enter as many events as I got money for. I'm a gambler."

The other man reached into his breast pocket for another cigarette, smiling with self-satisfaction. "That figures. You was entered in every contest yesterday. Even your roping was smooth as wind. You woulda won that if your hazer hadn't screwed up."

"What's your point, Marty?"

"I was talking about a job."

"Not interested."

Marty lit up. "You got no need of money, hey? Yesterday's puny winnings won't get you far."

Mitzy had come to stand by Kirk's chair; he petted her idly as they talked. "Yesterday's winnings are already gone," he grinned. "I told you, I'm a gambler. Though I've got to say my luck lately has been slime rotten. Would you happen to know a poker game that'll give credit?"

"Credit on what? You ain't got nothing, have you?"

"I got a little in wages. And another rodeo coming up in a couple weeks."

"That ain't good enough, Hawthorne. If you're smart you'll listen me out on this job offer. I can put you in touch with some real money, real soon."

The wooden rocking chair squeaked when Kirk leaned forward in it, resting his elbows on his knees. He looked down at his own bare feet. "Real money, huh? To me that translates as real risk."

"You ain't a man who's never flirted with risk, I'm sure enough of that."

Kirk's broad shoulders heaved in a sigh. He feigned deep thought. "My main interest is getting out of this valley."

"And going where?"

He shrugged. "Haven't decided."

Marty leaned back, curling his toes and puffing on his cigarette, a mischievous smile forming on his lips. "You're running from something, ain't you, Hawthorne? Something you done that ain't caught up with you yet?"

Kirk looked at him with a threatening scowl to let him know he was now overstepping his bounds. He meant to convince the man that what he guessed was true—that Kirk was, indeed, afoul of the law.

Marty drew back. "Look. This work ain't in the valley necessarily, but that doesn't mean you'd have to be gone a lot. It wouldn't interfere that much with your job here at Neilson's. Like I said, it's part-time. Temporary if you like. And don't tell me you got no interest in earning money."

"I'm not telling you that."

"Good. Then we're talking the same language. You're experienced in what we want, and in dodging the law—"

"Not without slipups," Kirk interrupted. He straightened, pressing back against the broken spindles of the old chair. "Okay, let's hear it. What's the job?"

"Not here. I got orders not to discuss it here. There's an old horse barn out on the Kendall property, down on the river. That's where we meet sometimes. I'll give you directions. Come down there tomorrow night and I'll introduce you to a couple other guys and we'll talk."

"On the river? If it's still raining like this tomorrow night, I'm not going out to some leaky horse barn on the river."

"It won't be raining tomorrow night. Weather forecast is clear. Are you gonna be there or not?"

"Okay. But only to listen."

"I guess that's fair enough."

Marty Schock set down the empty coffee mug and stood up, keeping wary eyes on the dog. With hurried, grunted-out directions to the horse barn on the Big Beaver River, he pulled on his boots.

"I need a lift out there," Kirk said with irritation, as if he'd expected Marty to know that.

"You ain't got no wheels? How come? What'd you come to town in?"

"A truck that wasn't mine."

"Hell." The other man grinned. "Okay, then, I'll pick you up out on the road at nine o'clock. If anybody asks, we've got a poker game." He exited with a handshake and a smile.

They had taken the bait, Kirk thought with a satisfied smile as he picked up his guitar again, in the bedroom. There was no question in his mind. Everything fit. The waiting was over.

THE BIG BEAVER was not a free-flowing river but a river made of channels and islands with thick vegetation. Clouds covered a pale moon so there was no light to guide them. Marty led the way, shining the beam of a very small flashlight in front of him. Leaves rustled in the dense river growth overhead and around them. Night-lurking insects buzzed and shrieked. A bullfrog was croaking loudly from the dark shore and was answered by another. They crossed over a makeshift bridge—one large plank laid across a narrow channel of water.

"I hate this place," Marty muttered. "There's snakes in here. Water moccasins."

"Why'd you choose it, then?" Kirk asked from behind him, trying to stay on the dry path with barely enough light to see where he was stepping.

"I didn't choose it. The boss did."

"Who's your boss?"

"Can't tell you that," the voice in the darkness answered. "Nobody knows that but me."

"You mean I'm not going to meet the guy you want me to work for?"

"Nope. He don't need to be here. Me and three other guys will explain all that's necessary for you to know about the job."

"I don't like the sound of this, Marty. I've just changed my mind. I'm going back."

"No, you ain't, because I'm your ride, remember? All you got to do is listen. Is that so tough?"

"No. I guess not. But listen is *all* the hell I'm gonna do. Let's get it real clear now, so everybody understands that."

"Fine. Then it'll be up to you if you want to turn down money like this after you hear us out."

They reached the barn, which was no better than a shack, leaning and worn. With eyes adjusted now to darkness, Kirk could see its uneven shape against patches of dark-gray sky showing through overhanging branches. Weak yellow light was glowing out from cracks in the shed.

Three men sat playing cards around a plank table by the light of a kerosene lantern. Smoke from their cigarettes hung in the air. They looked up without curiosity as Marty entered.

"Well, I brung him," Marty said, pulling the only extra chair up to the table, leaving Kirk standing.

Kirk eyed each man individually. Two of them he'd seen at the rodeo. The third was a stranger. One man stood up and offered him a cigarette. Kirk, who seldom smoked, accepted it and a light.

They produced a whisky bottle. "Want a drink?"

"No, thanks. I didn't come here for socializing."

"Hawthorne ain't real social," Marty confirmed. "So. Let's get down to business. This here is Rex, John and Smokey. The reason we came here is so they could meet you in person. If any of them decides he don't want to work with you, the deal's off."

"There is no deal," Kirk said.

"Right. There ain't, yet. But here's what it is. Your job would involve transporting livestock using portable loading chutes—"

Kirk scowled. His jaw clenched. "Whoa! Hang on there, cowboy! That's got a real nasty sound to it. I've been in some questionable situations in my time, but I've never messed around with stealing livestock!"

"Did I say you'd be stealing anything? You let me worry about where the critters come from. All you gotta do is transfer them from one vehicle to another, off-load and on-load."

Kirk threw down his cigarette and stepped on it. "Not interested."

The man called Smokey took a swallow of whiskey and wiped his hand across his mouth. "You know where else a drifter like you can pick up a thousand bucks for two hours' work?"

Kirk squinted down at him, his interest apparently renewed. "Nobody pays that kind of money."

"To a man who can handle any kind of a situation with livestock in the dark, our boss will pay it."

Kirk looked at Marty quizzically.

He smiled. "Smokey ain't lying. You interested now, Hawthorne?"

Kirk looked from one man to the other. All four were young—under forty—and all ranch hands, he assumed. All were wearing expensive boots. "I might be interested," he answered carefully. "That is, if I knew the name of the man I'd be working for."

"You'd be taking orders from me," Marty said.

"I get it. The guy who's running this operation keeps his identity secret so if any of us gets caught we can't rat. No plea bargains. He's protected."

"You got it. But our pay is good. You just have to complete your work, collect your money, and that's it. Somebody else takes over from there, with his part. You worried about getting caught?"

Kirk's lips tightened. "Not particularly. I told you, I'm a gambling man."

Rex pushed back his chair. "Does that mean you're in with us, Hawthorne?"

"I guess maybe it does. I'll admit, it's a hard offer to resist."

Smokey, a short, mustached cowboy who wore a hat low over his eyes, studied Kirk for a full ten seconds. "Stay sober in public," he said. "That's one rule we got among the lot of us."

Kirk grinned. "Sounds sensible to me."

The men, one by one, shook his hand and settled back down to their card game as if they'd been discussing the weather. Kirk watched them closely, listening to their conversation, while he was dealt a hand on credit. He became convinced that Marty had told the truth when he said none of the others knew whom they were working for. They didn't discuss the work at all, except now and again to remark about this thing or that thing they wanted to buy with the windfall of their earnings. Marty was closemouthed and somewhat aloof, the unchallenged leader of the group.

It would take some time, Kirk realized, to crack the cover of silence. But there would be some way to do it, to find out who the head of the rustling ring was. There was always a way. . . .

He played his cards close to his chest, betting recklessly. And every moment, he listened.

5

WATCHING THE LATE AFTERNOON become soft blue twilight, Beth drove home thirty-five miles along a country road from a ranch where she had been inspecting brands for a private sale. Vaguely she was aware that something within her had changed. Her secret thoughts spun a web around her, entangling her, ensnaring her. Lulled by the warmth inside her four-wheel-drive pickup, the purring of the engine and the ribbon of nearly empty road before her, she couldn't hold back her thoughts of one man.

She didn't want to think about him. It was foolish to be so dazzled by him. Drifters keep drifting; she knew that. Kirk Hawthorne would drift away, too, on the same restless winds that brought him. That is, unless he was sentenced to a jail term here in Prairie Hills, which seemed all too likely.

This was the most dominating and disturbing thought of all. Locking Kirk in prison would be like caging a wild animal. Beth strongly sensed that he was most at home in the vast expanse of hills. He had admitted to her that he couldn't stand still for long or stay in one place. Prison would be a harsh punishment for his crimes, whatever they were. Beth doubted she'd have had the courage to ask him what the charges were against him, if she were ever to see him again. No doubt it would all be in the newspaper, anyway, when his hearing came up.

Or his trial. It wouldn't be wise to visit him in prison. Being friendly with a stranger at a dance was one thing, but her visiting the prison would have the effect of throwing gasoline on a fire. The gossip would flame out of control. Lila—and Theo, too—would understandably be embarrassed.

So she wouldn't see him. She had to let the sediment of her secret thoughts settle, to become dry gray dust and blow away. She had to.

But later. Not today. Kirk was still free to feel the freshness of the air today and to watch the evening sun go down. The hills were brushed with pink light that splashed on high-blowing clouds above, making waves and scallops of color across the entire western sky. Summer twilight—the sweetest, softest time of day, when thoughts wandered often too far and dreams found marl to grow in.

Dreams and a harvest of intuitive whispers. Some secret surrounded Kirk; Beth was certain he was more than he appeared to be. His manners were just slightly too polished, his speech too educated, his wit too keen. Maybe he was running from something. Or searching for something. . . . Certainly, he was hiding something; during their conversation at the dance he'd volunteered so little about himself.

He didn't try to pretend he was anything other than a drifter—restless, rebellious, even treacherous. But who he really was remained untold. The man underneath, the man who had become a renegade, had secrets, dark secrets. She had felt the darkness.

THE FOLLOWING WEEK Kirk was summoned by Marty Schock in the middle of the night. He saddled one of Neilson's horses and rode out to a designated place, where he was met by Marty in a pickup truck. They drove to a thick grove of trees somewhere south of town where a livestock trailer was parked. Beside it was a large flatbed truck.

"It's just you and me," Marty explained. "Just you and me and one devilish mean Hereford bull that don't want no part of that trailer. I brung an extra pair of leather gloves so you won't get rope burn."

It took two ropes and the strength of two powerful men to convince the bull he was going to get into the trailer. Kirk came away with bruises on his legs and no more information than he'd had before about Marty's boss.

All efforts to win Marty's confidence had failed so far. The man protected his boss's identity with his life. There was going to be no other choice but to follow him, and when a man lived and worked mostly under open sky, that wasn't going to be easy. Getting impatient, having to be a part of more stealing, Kirk pondered the challenge, determined he was going to meet it, one way or another.

Riding back to the Neilson ranch on horseback, he followed the deserted dusty road by the light of the moon. His path took him past a small lake where the fluting of frogs and crickets rose up on the night air. There was no breeze; he found himself slapping at mosquitoes. He thought about the bull he and Marty had just done battle with. In the dark he hadn't been able to see the brand, but it wasn't important because an animal as valuable as that would be reported stolen within hours. It gave him a helpless feeling to know all he could do was make out a detailed report to slip to the sheriff. It would give him pleasure to arrest Marty for his part in this rustling, but far more pleasure to find the man who was behind all this.

The Hereford bull was probably on his way to Wyoming to be sold, but Kirk didn't want to think about that now. Riding back in the moonlight, his thoughts drifted again to Beth. First he had tried not to think about her, but images of her were never far under the surface of his conscious thoughts. In the shadows and the music of the night, they emerged vivid and beautiful.

Beautiful, he thought. She was so beautiful she seemed beyond the reach of any ordinary man. And he was only that—an ordinary man. She liked him, though; he could tell. Even believing he was a criminal, she liked him. This might have been encouraging were he free from the restraints of deceit. But he was not free. There was a job to do. Nothing could stand in the way of his duty, not even a woman like Beth.

Furthermore, any association with him might endanger her. He didn't know yet with whom he was dealing, except that all of them, boss and crew alike, were criminals. Risk takers. Should they find out he was crossing them, there was no predicting what might come down, and he didn't want Beth in the middle.

He smiled to himself and patted his horse. "As if I had to worry about it," he told his companion, who was walking at a faster pace now that the corrals of home were near. "As if the lady would so much as look at me now that she knows what I am.

"I can't tell her who I really am," he complained aloud to the horse. "I wonder, though—if I could tell her—how much difference it would make."

MORNING CAME EARLY to the hills because there was nothing, not even a tree, to block the rays of rising sun. The eastern sky on this particular morning was orange red, turning gradually to pink and then to yellow. By the time it was light enough to see, Kirk was in the hill pastures working on a sagging fence.

He was sick to death of this job, bored with mending fences, but at least he could enjoy the solitude of the hill pastures. There hadn't been enough solitude in his life for the past few years, he reflected, not since he'd taken the job in law enforcement. Perhaps he'd made a mistake not staying on the ranch with his brother. But it had been *too* solitary then, after life on the rodeo circuit and after his divorce from Candy. He hadn't wanted that much time to himself or too much time to think.

Things had changed. He didn't hurt anymore or need the stimulation of danger. There were moments when he felt a certain emptiness, though, when he felt something was missing from his life. Those times came with tenuous yearnings for the one thing he didn't have: warmth. The warmth of a woman's love.

His glove caught on a wicked barb while he was tightening the wire. Through the leather he felt the sharp, painful stab. Swearing, Kirk pulled off the glove and sucked at the trickle of blood on the palm of his hand. Only then did he notice a white horse approaching from the southwest. The horse was easily identifiable. So was its rider.

Appearing so slight on the large horse, with her dark hair flowing freely, was Beth. Kirk shaded his eyes and stood quite still, watching her grow nearer, clearer. She was wearing blue jeans and a yellow shirt. The white mane of her horse waved like silk. Kirk thought of the silkiness of Beth's hair when it had brushed against his throat as they danced. He remembered her perfume.

She reined in White Cloud to a stop. "I wondered if it was you."

"Disappointed?"

"Not in the slightest." She smiled.

He smiled back. "Are you out for a pleasure ride this early in the morning?"

"Good heavens, it isn't early for me. It rained last night," she added, as though it should mean something to him.

"Yeah. I realize that. I can't stay ahead of the leaks in the roof. Told Tom this morning that pouring tar on the leaks is an endless job. I'll have to put a whole new roof on that dilapidated house   be prepared to drown in my bed." He sucked at the wound on his hand again while he looked at her, wondering why she'd mentioned last night's rain when it rained often this time of year. "The downpour left the air fresh, anyhow," he offered.

"It pounded the sand hard in the blow—that eroded area northwest of the windmill. Which means conditions are perfect for finding arrowheads."

Surprised, he asked, "You rode up here this morning to hunt arrowheads?"

"It's one of my favorite things. You should see my collection. One of the best in the state, they say. And all the arrowheads are from Thistle County, every one. Mornings like this, after a rain, are the best time to look. What's wrong with your hand?"

"Nothing much. I just hooked it on the barbed wire. These are the meanest cursed barbs I've seen in my life. Where'd this wire come from, anyhow?"

"It's really old. Been here since I can remember." She jumped down nimbly from her horse and took Kirk's hand in hers, inspecting the still-bleeding wound. Pulling a clean tissue from her back pocket, she began dabbing at it gently. "I hope your tetanus shots are up-to-date."

He winced. "Did you ever see a man die of lock-jaw?"

"No! Have you?"

"When I was a little kid one of my dad's friends died of it. I wasn't there, but the cowboys talked about it for months—how his jaws really did lock and how he could've lived and not gone through all that hell but for the trouble of one thin needle. I never forgot that. Tetanus is one thing I'll admit to being scared of."

"It's hard to imagine you being scared of anything."

He grinned, allowing her to inspect his wound. "Pretty women scare me, too."

"That's not easy to believe, either. I should think it would be the other way around."

He caught her gaze when she looked up. "You're not afraid of me, are you?"

"Me?"

"Are you?"

"I'm not . . . not sure."

"Why would you be?" He blinked. "Oh, hell, by now you know I'm a thief, huh, since everybody in this half of the county knows? But I don't steal women. I'm not that good at my craft."

"You're being very sarcastically defensive," she said, "when there's no cause to be. I haven't given you cause."

"No," he agreed. "You haven't."

She pressed the tissue to his hand. "This really is a deep cut. How did you do it?"

"Carelessness. There was a rabbit scampering down the hillside. I was looking at him instead of the wire."

Beth smiled softly. "You enjoy the wildlife, don't you?"

This gentle observation caught him off guard. He paused and simply nodded, and for a moment his thoughts seemed to drift away.

"You're not going to be able to do much work with this hand."

"Not until it stops bleeding and throbbing. Arrow-head hunting sounds a lot more interesting than mending fences, anyhow. Any objections if I come along to the blow with you?"

Beth hesitated. Her head told her there was something forbidden, dangerous, about this man because he was a criminal, but nothing else inside her seemed to want to go along with that conviction. Her heart didn't; in all the heart ways, she liked him very much. Even her instincts, on which she relied a great deal, didn't hesitate. Only her head did, and here in the free hills there was really no way to keep him from riding to the blow-out if he wanted to. They wouldn't be hunting very near each other, anyhow; the blowout was huge.

"Be my guest," she answered, knowing her reckless-ness would shock Theo and Lila. Kirk had already told her she had nothing to fear from him, and gazing at his eyes, she believed him.

He smiled and pulled on his glove carefully over the folded tissue to hold it in place. Then he untied a small canteen from the side of his saddlebag and offered her a drink. She shook her head and watched as he un-screwed the cap and drank thirstily, his head back, his Adam's apple bobbing with each swallow.

Beth mounted and began riding along the fence in the direction of the blow. In moments he was alongside her on the sorrel he usually rode, but on Neilson's side of the barbed wire. When they reached the wire gate, she waited while he crossed through.

"Why is this large eroded area here in the middle of the grassland?" he asked.

"During World War I, when everybody was into planting victory gardens, this area was plowed up for corn. The soil was much too sandy for growing any-thing but grass; I can't believe no one figured that out before they tried it. Anyhow, the natural prairie grass never rooted here again and year after year the sand just keeps eroding. Luckily the area has never gotten much bigger. We've always called it a blow, because the sand blows when the wind is strong. After a rainstorm, it's packed down pretty well and then arrowheads are easy to see."

There was a post that Beth's father had erected in the sand, to which they tied the horses. She became animated in her excitement, rushing ahead toward a scattering of small stones on the edge of the blow.

"I always look here first," she said. "The Indians had a fire pit here once." She kicked at the stones with the toe of her boot. "Look! Here's a piece."

She turned over the dark-gray stone in her palm, exposing clear chippings done with a tool. "Let's have a competition, Kirk! The first one who finds a whole arrowhead is the winner."

"Besides the arrowhead, what's the prize for winning?"

"I don't know. What should it be?"

He'd have liked to say dinner at the best steak house in town, but that suggestion would have been out of line. He doubted Beth Connor would want to be seen with him in public again, now that she knew who he was. He gazed down at her—her hair shining in the sun and blowing softly in the breeze, her eyes filled with excitement over the arrowheads.

But there was something more in her eyes that unnerved Kirk, threatened to pull at his insides almost the way he plucked at guitar strings to make them sing. He heard his own voice answering, "If I win the competition, I get to kiss you."

Beth blinked, caught off guard by his astounding proposition. Her heart fluttered wildly. Quickly she rallied and rose to the challenge. "And if I win?"

"You get to kiss me."

She simply looked at him with an expression he couldn't identify, not quite curiosity and not quite mischief. Likely it was a combination of many things—all unspoken but not all new.

He hadn't really meant to say it. Certainly he hadn't *planned* to. But seeing her beauty in the sunshine in this lonely place, he hadn't been able to stop himself. Silence hung between them for a few seconds. She seemed to be trying to take in the full implication of his challenge. His words had been light, careless. His eyes were not laughing, though.

Finally she answered both this stranger and her fluttering heart. "Okay, cowboy! It's a deal."

They began a diligent search, moving in separate directions. Beth found herself thinking less about arrowheads than about the bargain she had made with Kirk Hawthorne.

She had given a truthful answer when he'd asked if she was afraid of him, but she couldn't define the basis of her fear. Perhaps it was because he was socially off-limits. He'd chosen to walk a path of crime and now faced prison. Or perhaps it was because he was so different from any other man she'd ever known and she couldn't understand him. Was it the mystery surrounding him—his secrets? Then again, it might have been the untamable fluttering of her own heart that frightened her.

The eroded area she called a blow was large. Beth had the advantage of familiarity, knowing where the ground might be hardest packed, but it was only a slight advantage because arrowheads were everywhere, all over the hills. Finding them in the buff-colored sand wasn't easy. The hooves of cattle had broken many.

Fresh hoofprints showed cattle had walked over the blow already this morning.

The sand was too soft to echo footsteps, and the hills were so quiet that hidden insects seemed to be playing a symphony. For a time Kirk was out of sight, on the other side of a small rise. Beth found one very large piece of what might have been a tomahawk, but she didn't find an unbroken arrowhead. When she caught sight of Kirk again—his light-blue shirt against the blue-white air of the lengthening morning—he was walking toward her.

"Any luck?"

She shook her head. "You?"

He shrugged. "I don't know about you, but I'm getting hot, and my horse is thirsty. I'm heading for the windmill. Are you ready to give this up?"

"I guess so. I've already searched out all my favorite spots."

No winner. Disappointment stung her—there was no denying it to herself—but at the same time, the regret came with a stroke of relief. Kirk didn't seem unduly bothered; it was only a game, after all.

Riding back, he reined in his horse on the crest of a hill and looked out across the pasture at an area that was dotted with a hundred little mounds of sand. "Prairie dogs," he said.

"Yes. It's better if we go around them. This prairie-dog town is larger than it looks." It wasn't safe for the horses here; he would know that as well as she did. There were too many holes to step in. "Rattlesnakes are pretty thick here, too. And owls, using the prairie-dog holes for nesting."

"Yeah. Good hunting ground for the coyotes." He turned the reins of his horse.

They circled the "town" and, under sky that stretched forever, rode in silence until they reached the windmill. Kirk dismounted first and led his horse to the tank. Beth and White Cloud were right behind him. She cupped her hands at the pipe where water was pumping in and leaned over to drink. Kirk did the same and splashed water over his face, drying it with his shirt-sleeve. Brushing back damp hair he commented, "The sun makes me thirsty."

The windmill was creaking its familiar melancholy song, a song like no other in the world, made more melancholy because it was the only sound around them, save for the buzzing flies and the jingle of water trickling from the pipe into the tank.

Kirk said, "This reminds me of old times. Reminds me of the day we met."

Beth had been remembering that day, too, and at his mention of it, she flushed.

"You're blushing," he said.

Lowering her gaze from his eyes didn't help because she found herself looking at jeans that hugged his husky thighs; they were unnervingly tight. Sun glinted from his silver belt buckle; obviously he'd won it in some rodeo somewhere... Involuntarily, she closed her eyes.

"It's not that bad, is it?" he asked.

"What?"

"The memory of the first time you saw me."

She swallowed and couldn't answer, embarrassed because she couldn't answer. He was teasing her again, deliberately flustering her. Desperately she fished for a

retort, to give him measure for measure, but none
came.

And then, surprisingly, he offered in a husky voice,
"I'm sorry."

"For...what?"

"For embarrassing you."

Beth recovered her wit. "Yeah. Trying to make me
remember. But you don't have to try, I assure you."

"I suspected as much."

"Oh? Why? Conceit?"

"Probably."

She laughed softly and allowed herself to look at him
again. He was the one who should have been embarrassed. He wasn't; not the least bit. Not now, anyway.
His eyes—those silver-blue eyes that had been so angry the last time she'd been here with him at this windmill—were soft now. More than softness, there was
tenderness in his gaze.

Beth experienced the same sensation she had felt at
the rodeo when he'd looked at her—a weakness in her
knees, a strange catch in her throat. He stepped nearer,
so near she felt as if she had moved into the warm
shadows of his eyes.

He had taken the glove from his cut hand half an hour
ago, when the bleeding had stopped. Now he reached
his good hand into the breast pocket of his shirt, then
held out the palm of his hand to her. Beth gasped.
There, cold and hard and gleaming in the sun, lay an
arrowhead! It was creamy white with blue at the tip, at
least two inches long and perfectly preserved.

She thrilled at the beauty of it. "I thought you didn't
find one!"

"I didn't say that."

"Why didn't you tell me?"

"Because I was hot and thirsty. I didn't want to . . . collect my reward just then. Now I do."

6

HE PRESSED THE ARROWHEAD into her hand. She felt his shirt brush against her chest, felt the sensation of his arms around her, felt his breath and then his lips. His touch was gentle—his arms, his lips—gentle, almost careful. Careful to be sure she wouldn't back away, gentle to be sure she wasn't frightened.

The world spun around her the way the rotors of the windmill spun shadows on the pallid sand as she accepted his kiss, touching his neck, reaching her arms around him, feeling his embrace tighten in response to the heated sensation of her lips on his.

The kiss deepened until awareness of everything else dissolved, until in all the world there were only the two of them, nothing else, not space, not time. Beth experienced a flood of emotion that left her weightless and breathless, and when finally Kirk pulled back it seemed to her it was so far back—those few small inches—that something had been torn away from her, perhaps forever.

Tears filled her eyes; she couldn't stop them. She stared at him for some moments before she found her trembling voice. "Kirk, who are you?"

His expression abruptly changed, suddenly hardened, and a frown creased his brow. He sucked in his breath, as if in a sigh that he didn't allow to escape.

"I'm just..." he said awkwardly, his voice still husky from the kiss, "just a guy...." He paused for a long time before he added, "A man who thinks you're very... beautiful."

He appeared blurry through her tears, but Beth continued to look at him, not comprehending. He wouldn't tell her who he was, not now, probably not ever. He harbored some deep dark secret; she felt it even more strongly now with his evasive answer than she had before. There had been no point at all in asking.

Kirk seemed to sense her frustration. The sigh he had restrained came now, and for a second or two his eyes closed. "I wish I were the wind," he said. "Because the wind can dry your tears and I can't."

His finger touched a tear that stained her cheek, a tear she had scarcely felt. Then he hugged her close to him as he might have held a child after a bad dream. He simply held her. She could feel the beating of his heart behind the hard muscles of his chest and feel the material of his shirt against her cheek.

"I'm not crying," she insisted. "I was only—"

"I know."

"You know what?"

"I know you're confused about me. I'm sorry. I didn't . . . plan this, and neither did you."

"No one ever kissed me like that in my life."

"No one ever kissed me like that, either." A little sound of frustration came from his chest, half moan, half grunt. "I wish . . ." he began, and then abruptly stopped.

She looked up at him quizzically, her hand on his chest. *I wish, too,* she thought. How she wished things were different, wished this man could be more than a passing moment in her life, wished he was not . . . who he was.

As if he was reading her thoughts, he said, "Beth, you're out of my reach and you know it. It wouldn't do for us to be seen in public together again."

"Why? Are you ashamed of me?"

He laughed and touched her chin. "At this moment, I wish you were a bad and bawdy lady fit for the likes of me. You're not, though. You're the kind of girl a man. . . ." Once more he stopped himself.

She waited.

He finished lamely. " . . . a man like me has no business with."

She knew that wasn't what he'd originally intended to say. She whispered, "Perhaps you're right," and pulled away.

"Yeah, damn it, I'm right."

Beth opened her hand and held out to him the white arrowhead, warm and shining with the moisture of her skin. "This is yours."

"Nah, keep it. It's yours." He took the reins of his horse from the windmill strut. "Wouldn't it be a kick to know who the Indian was who held that arrowhead last and what he was doing with it at the time? Hunting rabbits, maybe, or birds, or maybe he just lost it there on the sand."

Beth smiled. "That's exactly what I wonder every time I find one. I wish this arrowhead could talk and tell us what was going on around here when it fell in the grass."

He laughed. "I'm glad the little thing *can't* talk. It might have too much to say about today."

Another secret, Beth thought as she mounted her horse. "Are you going back to the blow?"

"No. I've got work to finish."

"How's your hand?"

On his horse, he looked at the hand as though he'd forgotten it was hurt. Flexing his fingers, he winced slightly. "It's okay. It's nothing." The horse was eager to move; Kirk reined him in. "Beth...."

"Yes?"

"Thanks . . . for dropping by my fence."

"Anytime." She turned toward home.

The lonely hills spread out from them, separating them. Beth turned back once to see him cantering across the pasture. She gave rein to White Cloud and felt the rough edges of the arrowhead in her hand. The wind blew her hair and dried the unwanted tear of frustration that found its way down her cheek. *I wish I were the wind*, he'd said to her with his eyes closed to the sun and to her need for answers.

AS SHE WAS TURNING into the gate at the Circle C, the mail truck stopped and waited for her. The mailman, dressed in jeans and a straw cowboy hat, smiled a greeting. "This your day off, Beth?"

"Yes. I usually take Mondays off, unless something comes up to prevent it." She reached down for the small stack of mail. "I'll take that in, Henry. How's your wife? Isn't the baby due anytime now?"

He grinned. "Yep, any day. Edith Miller says it's gonna be a boy for sure, and Edith's always right, so everybody says."

"She always is. Let me know if there's anything I can help with."

"We'll do that, Beth. Thanks." He waved as he put the truck in gear.

Beth unsaddled her horse in the barn and poured a little crushed corn into a feed box for him before she went into the kitchen door at the side of the house. The house was silent, but there was a pot of coffee on the stove. Evidently Lila and Theo were out, as usual.

Over a cup of black coffee, she sat down to sort through the mail. A Canadian postage stamp caught her eye. The letter, addressed to Theo, looked for all the world like a bank statement. Odd, she thought, that Theo would have an account in a Canadian bank and never have mentioned it. But he had traveled a great deal before she'd met him and had lived several years overseas. There were many things about him she didn't know.

Dismissing the twinge of curiosity, she stacked the letter with the others and tried to read her own mail, having to cope with the realization that, for the morning at least, she'd lost her ability to concentrate. Kirk's face was before her like an apparition, the feel of his lips on hers still warm. His eyes, his smile, the sight of him riding away. . . And still with her was the vivid picture of him in handcuffs, always there to remind her of what she wanted to forget.

Finishing her coffee, she gathered up the mail, left Lila's letters on the hall table and started for Theo's office at the far end of the house, intending to leave his mail on his desk. His voice reached into the long hallway through the almost-closed door. Theo wasn't out, after all. He was on the phone.

"I don't care where the bed is now! I want it up there by the twenty-first. No, damn it, I said the twenty-first!" An impatient pause. "They've got a branding scheduled, you idiot! I'm not going to discuss it now." A short silence, then a rasp. "Later. I'll meet you. Fine. Okay. Be on time, then."

Beth paused outside the door, confused. Theo's telephone conversation didn't make any sense. What did he mean he had a branding schedule? They weren't due to brand until September. What "bed" was he talking about? Or maybe she hadn't heard him right. Of course she'd heard him; she was standing within ten feet of him.

She entered his office clearing her throat. Theo looked up at his stepsister, startled.

"Hi, Beth! I thought you'd be out hunting arrowheads this morning."

"I have been. I'm back."

"Any luck?"

She took the arrowhead from her pocket and held it out for him to see.

He picked it up and examined it. "It's a good one. Unusual color, isn't it?"

"Sort of. I didn't mean to disturb your work, Theo. I was just bringing your mail by."

"Since when would the pretty face of my sister disturb me?" He began swiftly glancing through the stack of mail.

"Do you have an account in a Canadian bank?" she asked.

One eyebrow raised with his glance, over the envelope in question. He slapped it against his wrist and smiled. "Just more junk mail. I don't know how I get on all these mailing lists."

His beard made it difficult sometimes to read the expression on Theo's attractive face, so her attention tended to focus on his blue eyes. His eyes were smiling, but the left one was squinting slightly, as it always did when he was bothered about something. Beth had never seen him without the beard, and she was sometimes curious as to why he wore it when his features looked so nearly perfect. She couldn't shake the feeling that what bothered him now, causing the left eye to squint, was the chance she might have overheard his telephone conversation.

Might their neighbors have branding plans she didn't know about? Beth opened her mouth to ask him when a fragment of memory hit her like a stinging dart; Sheriff Ollie Arnold was certain that a flatbed truck was used by the rustlers to steal cattle. Surely when he'd said "bed," Theo couldn't have been referring to a truck!

Beth blinked, tossing her head as if to shake off the shivery murmurs of her cursed runaway imagination. She stared at her stepbrother blankly, her mouth open.

"What's the matter?" Theo rose, came around his desk and gently touched her forearm. "Why are you looking at me that way?"

"What way?" she asked, hearing her own voice squeak out flat and high. His left eye was squinting more noticeably now. He seemed to be looking through her, but at the same time his gaze was full of genuine concern. She was being silly, she thought. Silly and utterly paranoid!

All she had to do was ask him, to clear it all up, but to have Theo think she was meddling in his private affairs would be totally unacceptable. Even worse, for him to get the impression she somehow mistrusted him would be unfair and disloyal. She didn't mistrust him; there had never been any reason to. Ever. Theo's conversation could have meant any of a number of things, and a bed was not necessarily a truck.

The twenty-first, he had said. Whatever Theo had planned for the twenty-first was no concern of hers. Probably he was helping out on one of the neighboring ranches; it was common practice to help with branding. She wanted to ask, "Who was that on the phone just a minute ago?" but something stopped her. She couldn't throw off the coiling feeling of something wrong—something so wrong her insides had gone hollow.

Theo repeated, "What's the matter, Beth?"

"Nothing." She slid the arrowhead back into her pocket. "I'm just a little dizzy. It was hot in the hills this morning. It's going to be a scorcher. I should've worn a hat."

"Are you okay? Can I get you anything? Some ice water? Iced tea?"

She forced a smile. "No, really. I'm fine."

He sat down on the edge of his desk and smiled. "Have you seen any more of your infamous rodeo rider since the dance?"

"*My* infamous rodeo rider? If you mean Kirk Haw-thorne, yes, I saw him in the hills this morning. He was mending fences for Tom Neilson."

"Yeah? Has he gotten around to admitting to you that he's a blackguard and a rogue?"

Beth sputtered with laughter. "A what and a what? Good grief, Theo, what kind of stuff have you been reading lately?"

"Sherlock Holmes, my dear. And you haven't an-swered my question."

"The answer's yes. Kirk has admitted that he's a blackguard and a rogue, and it doesn't seem to bother him much."

His smile vanished. He looked at her with the same concern he'd had the other night at the dance. "How much does it bother *you*?"

"Why would it bother me?"

"Come on, honey girl, this is Theo you're talking to. I saw the look in your eyes the other morning when Mother was doing her spiel about gold-digging drift-ers. She was getting to you. You like him, don't you?"

Beth rubbed her arm self-consciously while she looked out the window at the horses pastured in the meadow. A blue jay, perched in the branches of a tall willow tree just outside the window, commanded her attention with his strange song. For a while she watched the bird. "It isn't important whether or not I like him, Theo. He is what he is, and I'm . . . what I am. I'm not stupid enough to get myself entangled with him."

His smile came easier than before. There was genu-ine affection in Theo's eyes, and the strange squint was gone. "I'm glad to hear you say that, Beth. I'd be lying if I said I hadn't been a little concerned. I'd hate like the devil to see you hurt."

"I'm not that vulnerable, nor that naive. You should have more faith in me, Theo."

"Hell, I've got faith in you! Just like I'd like to think you have faith in me. Families have to stick together, kid. I was prepared to face this bum and put him in his place if I had to, but hell, I knew down deep I wouldn't have to. You're too smart to get taken in."

Her voice dropped to almost a whisper. "He's just...a drifter...."

She turned to leave, still feeling the effects of that drifter's kiss.

"I'm going to be out most of the day," Theo said. "See you at dinner tonight."

"Right. Okay...."

He was still sitting on the edge of his desk when she left the room. Feeling somewhat giddy from her morning in the hills, Beth left the house by the kitchen door and walked down a lane of willow trees toward the pond that had been her favorite childhood retreat. Her dog, James, always eager for a romp, joined her, running ahead, sniffing the trails of rabbits and squirrels.

The frogs' night-fluting voices were still now, in midmorning. It was the time for bird songs instead, songs Beth knew by heart, songs that filled her memories as far back as memory could take her. The songs of the birds were happy and sad at the same time. Kirk had seemed surprised when she'd observed that he was fascinated by the animals of the wilderness, as if he'd never given any thought to his fascination. Yet the hawk standing on the wind and the rabbit scampering over the hills had distracted him from the heavier moments of his day and given him cause for wonder.

Perhaps he was a man of nature's world, not a man's, and consciously or unconsciously cared more for nature's rules than for those of human society. Beth had sensed his closeness to nature in a hundred little ways when they were in the hills. He'd given little attention to the painful sting of a horsefly on his arm. He'd ridden toward the sun without squinting. He'd repeatedly glanced toward the prairie-dog settlement in hopes of seeing one of the elusive little creatures that stayed indoors with the warning of the horses' hooves upon the slope.

Sitting on a sandy bank beside the pond, chin in her palms, Beth reflected on the surprises of the morning. Finding Kirk in the hills again. Finding the heat of his mouth against her own. Feeling his heartbeat against her own. And afterward, Theo's letter from a bank in Canada, which did not look like junk mail. And Theo's strangely unnerving conversation on the phone.

She knew, truly, so little about her stepbrother. Until he and his young Australian wife had come to live at the Circle C soon after Beth's father had died, she'd never met him. He'd been working at a station in the Australian outback for several years, and he knew horses and cattle as well as any man she'd ever known. Beth had liked his wife, Mary, very much but had never been able to get close to her. Four months after they'd come to America Mary had left Theo for reasons she'd never shared with any of them except her husband, and he was closemouthed about it. Beth had always assumed the girl had been homesick, because she'd returned to Australia. Theo never spoke of her anymore; it was as if Mary had never been there at all.

Beth was glad Theo had come. She was unable to run a big ranch alone and would have had to hire someone if it hadn't been for him. It had all happened so easily, so naturally, the way things do when they are meant to be. She respected his business sense and his knowledge of livestock; under their joint management they had done well. And thanks to her trust in Theo, she could keep her demanding job as brand inspector, which she loved.

In the beginning Beth thought she sensed some resentment from Theo that she had inherited the ranch in its entirety—none had gone to Lila. She'd seen that strange squint in his eye sometimes. But Theo knew a good thing, too, when it came his way. He and Lila had a large herd and use of the pastureland and half of the enormous house, as Beth had decided to use just the upstairs for herself. The resentment faded, if indeed it had ever been there at all. The three of them, she and Theo and Lila, worked well together and played well together. Like any other family.

She threw a stone into the still, moss-edged water of the pond. Strangely, the ripples it created seemed to take the shape of an arrowhead. Ripples couldn't do that, she reflected dreamily; only her imagination could form an arrowhead from a scroll of curling ripples.

Nevertheless, the heat seemed to issue from the white arrowhead in her shirt pocket, creating a little glow against her breast. Beth took out the arrowhead once again and gazed at it for a long time, reliving the intimate moments it had given her—Kirk's excuse to kiss her. Strange that a chip of stone could exude such warmth—warmth from ten thousand days of summer rain and winter sun and secrets of long ago. Warmth from today's secret kiss that would stay in her heart forever.

Beth sighed, watching the ripples in the water flutter out to the shores and disappear, the way ripples of ecstasy disappear. She tried to force her thoughts from Kirk. *Do something,* she demanded of herself. *Try not to think of him!* This was her day off. She should be picking the ripe cucumbers in the garden or something, anything.

Heading back toward the house with the dog at her side and trying to set her mind on the watermelons and cucumbers in her garden, more disturbing thoughts began to needle her. The twenty-first, Theo had said with some kind of strange desperation in his voice. Desperation or anger or...or something. Something ominous. The date stuck in her head. What the devil could be so important to Theo about the twenty-first?

THE TOWN OF SIOUX SPRINGS was two hours from Prairie Hills. Beth was used to the drive because she worked at sales there several times a year. The livestock auction the following weekend was going to be a big one and a busy one because it fell on the weekend of the Sioux Springs Fair and Rodeo.

On Wednesday of that week she received an unexpected phone call at work. The moment she heard her name, she knew who the caller was. No other voice was that deep or that mysterious or that beautiful.

"Beth," he said. "I know we agreed to, uh, not to...socialize...but this is different. This is business."

Her pulse seemed to be throbbing in her ears, and she resented that fact. It wasn't fair for a man's voice to affect her this way. It wasn't fair for a *man* to affect her this way—to cause her heart to quicken and her knees to gel.

"I heard you were going to be inspecting brands at the sale in Sioux Springs this weekend."

"How did you hear that?"

"I asked around. There's a rodeo there, a big one. Big purse."

"Yes," she said in an unsteady voice, "I know. Are you going to enter?"

"I want to. But I don't have wheels. I'm not, uh, allowed to drive. I got this idea that since you're driving up there, maybe I could hitch a ride."

"Sure."

"Did you say sure?"

Beth smiled. "Why do you sound so surprised?"

"I expected you to hesitate and have to think about it—about what people would say."

"I don't generally worry about what people will say. You ought to know that. Anyway, I don't know any people in Sioux Springs, outside of the people at the auction barn."

"Good. Neither do I. When are you leaving?"

"Early Friday morning. About six."

"I'll be out on the road by the mailbox at six."

She could easily drive the half mile in from the road to Neilson's ranch house, then thought better of suggesting it. He was trying to spare her the embarrassment of being seen picking him up, and for that she probably ought to be grateful.

"All right. I'll be by Neilson's mailbox at six."

"Thanks, Beth. I appreciate this."

Kirk hung up the phone and walked out of the booth into the street. He had just come away from a meeting with Marty at the coffee shop in the bus depot, where he'd learned there was a group of unbranded calves waiting to be transported to the Sioux Springs sale from somewhere east of that town. Marty and his elusive boss had decided the rodeo was a good cover—the perfect excuse for Kirk to be there. He was to transfer the calves on Friday afternoon and someone else would take them to Saturday's sale. Marty assumed Kirk would jump at the chance to enter the rodeo for all three days, and Kirk went along with him. He didn't rodeo often anymore, but he still enjoyed the challenge.

So far in his dealings with Marty, Kirk hadn't been privy to any more than he already knew about the rustling operation. His job was to help disperse stolen cattle after the fact, so he hadn't been able to learn much. His plan to follow Marty and try to monitor his activities had presented obvious problems, as he'd predicted. So far he hadn't turned up a single clue, but it was still the only workable plan. Whether he liked it or not, Kirk had to call on the patience he'd learned as a lawman.

Riding over to Sioux Springs with Beth had been his own idea, one he hadn't mentioned to Marty. He'd merely said he'd hitchhike. Marty wasn't going to be working with him this time; someone else was going to meet him with the calves. This operation, Kirk realized more each day, was big and well organized. He figured there might be as many as a dozen people involved in various capacities.

He had been restless during the past week, thinking about the morning in the hills with Beth. Thinking about the way she had returned his kiss, her hands grasping his shoulders as though she was afraid of letting go. He remembered the feel of her nails pressing into his skin and the way her body had become weightless, her lips opening softly on his. At first, he'd sensed reluctance—fear—and then, with release of fear, a new acceptance of him.

It was a different kind of acceptance than he'd ever felt before in a kiss. There was a wildness in it. There was a wildness in *her* that was identifying with the forbidden presence of him. As if touching him was the same as touching fire or wind. As if together they *became* fire and wind. But they were not wind and fire, not good and evil; they were man and woman—nothing more, nothing less. Kirk couldn't forget that kiss, couldn't stop thinking about it, because it had changed something inside of him.

HE STOOD against the light of sunrise, a dark silhouette against the yellow sky. When Beth brought her pickup to a stop by the mailbox, he tossed a bedroll into the back of the truck and set his guitar case on the seat between them.

"Will this be in the way?"

"No." She smiled. "Is that all you have—just the bedroll and guitar?"

"What more does a man need in life than a change of clothes, a blanket and his guitar?"

The radio in the truck was on. Beth reached over and turned it off.

He asked, "Where do you stay in Sioux Springs?"

"There are only three motels in town. Two of them are very near the fairgrounds. I stay at one called the Lodge. It's pretty nice and not expensive."

"Would you have any objection to my bedding down in the back of the truck tonight?"

She glanced over at him. He was serious. "You want to sleep in the pickup?"

"I have to pay entry fees—can't afford the luxury of a motel. Anyway, I'm used to sleeping out under the stars. Done it all my life."

"For pleasure or necessity?"

"Both, I guess. Didn't you ever lie and watch the stars come out at night one by one?"

"Yes, I have done that, when I was young. Not for years, though."

"Hell, I still love it. I have the whole sky memorized. I remember when I was a little kid watching the sky and trying to understand why the brightest star moved and why sometimes this reddish star moved, too, while the others just stood there night after night. My dad told me I was looking at Venus and Mars and that they were planets, not stars. It took me quite a while to figure that out. I had to wait till I was old enough to read astronomy books."

"I've had the feeling ever since I've known you that you're well educated. I mean far beyond what most—" She hesitated.

He helped her. "Drifters?"

"Yeah, beyond what most drifters would be."

"What makes you think so?"

She smiled. "You're not that good at hiding it."

"Okay," he conceded. "Guilty."

"College?"

"Yeah."

"Where?"

"The University of Montana."

"I see."

"No, I don't think you do." His voice was teasing but gentle. "You can't understand why an educated man would become a bum."

"Well . . . actually, that is what I was wondering."

"I majored in bum. Bumology."

Beth laughed. "You're not going to tell me why, are you?"

"There's nothing to tell." Kirk seemed to be fishing for words. He was not comfortable with this subject, in spite of his offhand attitude. "I had . . . have certain ideals. Society has certain ideals. They're not the same. I can't live like other people do. I just choose to live my own way, that's all."

"You're not saying, anything," she replied. "And yet you are. I think all, uh, unconventional people feel something similar. Have you always been a rebel?"

"I don't know."

"You were married once. Do you have children?"

"No. Lord, no. Do I look like a father?"

"Why not? Do fathers have to look a certain way?"

He laughed. "I guess not. My old man looked like an old crusty cowboy."

"You talk about your dad a lot."

"Do I?"

"Is he still alive?"

"No. But I miss him."

"What about your mother?"

"My mother's a nice lady. In her eyes I can do no wrong." He shifted. "Why are we talking about me? It's dull talking about me."

"Depends on the point of view. I don't find it dull."

It was obvious to Beth that he wanted to change the drift of the conversation, but if he asked questions about her, he'd only be opening the door for questions back. He didn't want to talk about himself. Neither did she. It had been better in the hills, with just the two of them and nothing else but the grass and sky, nothing of society at all, as if it existed too far away to matter. Yes, it was better that way.

He may have been reading her mind, because he reached for his guitar case and said, "I'm better at playing than talking. Would you mind?"

"Of course not. I wish you would."

He snapped open the case, took out the instrument and settled back into the seat. It was an old guitar, scratched, well used but carefully polished. When Beth saw the make, she discovered a whole new dimension to this man. Only a serious musician would own such an expensive guitar.

Eyebrows raised she observed, "A Martin!"

He nodded. "I wouldn't trade this guitar for any horse living." He began to strum.

"The tone is beautiful!"

"Best I've ever heard, if you don't mind the bragging. I saved for five years for this thing. It's been bumped around like hell, but it sounds as good as it ever did." He looked at her. "You know guitars, huh? Do you play?"

"No. I wish I did. But I'm awfully good at listening."

"At singing, too?"

"I guess. Sometimes."

The sun was well up in the sky by now, reflecting off the glass and warming the pickup as he strummed. He hummed "Bobby McGee" along with his skilled accompaniment. Beth hummed along with him.

He picked a number of familiar melodies—some country, some pop tunes, folk ballads. He even lapsed smoothly into flamenco. His fingers flew over the strings.

"You're good!" she exclaimed.

"Thanks. Want anything special?"

She hadn't seemed to hear his bid for requests. "You're good at everything you do."

"Hell, not everything."

"What aren't you good at?"

He shrugged, still picking at the strings. "I'm not good at pretending I can forget the way you kissed me last week."

Beth riveted her eyes on the road. "Oh."

"Neither are you."

A long pause, filled only with his music, ensued.

"I know," she answered finally. "I'm never good at pretending."

"That's to your credit," he said, as if the same somehow didn't apply to him, which bothered her.

She listened to his humming. His voice embraced music naturally, and the sound was very sexy—so velvety and so deep.

"Sing something, Kirk."

He strummed softly, shifted his legs for more comfort and leaned his head back against the seat. Slowly the humming became words, and the song recognizable. She felt goose bumps rise on her skin, and a strange, sweet taste formed in her mouth. These would be treasured moments: the steady hum of the engine, the reflection of moving sun rays on the window and on his face, the sound of Kirk's deep voice, his music and a love song for her.

7

BETH COULD HAVE SWORN that the distance between Prairie Hills and Sioux Springs had shrunk. With Kirk strumming his guitar and the two of them remembering songs and chuckling when he forgot the lyrics and made up words of his own, the magic-filled minutes tumbled over one another somehow out of the context of time. With him, time took on a definition of its own and was not the same for her as time had ever been before.

They spent the hours playing and singing, because they couldn't talk—at least not about themselves. Kirk didn't want that and Beth once again wondered about the secrets that lurked in the shadows of his eyes. He was running from something, she decided. He was hiding from something. Perhaps from the truth. He seemed so reckless and carefree that Beth suffered a new jolt every time some small thing reminded her that he was awaiting trial—awaiting prison.

The buildings of Sioux Springs were already in view in the distance when a new fear rose to goad her. Would he run? Did he have permission to travel here, or was he using her as an escape? No one had seen them leave Prairie Hills together; Kirk had made certain of that. It had been his idea she not be seen with him again after their morning in the hills, so no one would think of them being together. If Kirk planned to jump bail, this was his perfect opportunity to do so!

Beth was engulfed by a wave of panic. It would make perfect sense that he had planned this secret excursion in order to jump bail here, over a hundred miles from Prairie Hills! How could she have been so naive! Fighting back tears, feeling foolish and used, she asked, "Kirk, when are you going back to Prairie Hills?"

"Whenever you are."

"Sunday."

"Before or after Sunday's rodeo?"

"When is Sunday's rodeo?"

"Afternoon. There are night performances tonight and tomorrow night and one in the afternoon on Sunday."

"You want to enter all three?"

He shrugged. "I might."

She smiled, feeling somewhat reassured. "Maybe I'll take in Sunday's rodeo, then."

"Great! That'd be great."

"I guess you'll find me."

"Huh?"

"Before we leave Sioux Springs to come home, I mean. You know the hotel here I'll be."

"Oh . . . yeah."

He seemed strangely preoccupied. His thoughts were partly elsewhere, his fingers plucking softly at the guitar strings. Her fear soared again. "Kirk?"

"Yeah?"

"You wouldn't . . . ?" She nearly choked on her own breath and couldn't say the words.

"I wouldn't what?"

Anything she said would not make the slightest difference, she knew. This was a man whose freedom was at stake. A few words from her wouldn't influence him one way or another, so why put herself on the line? If he had used her, it was already too late to do anything about it, short of reporting him to the sheriff. She couldn't do that; he hadn't jumped bail yet and there was absolutely no proof that he would. No, whatever she said wouldn't change anything now.

"Wouldn't what?" he repeated.

"Nothing."

He shrugged and gazed out the window. "Is this Sioux Springs?"

"Yes." Her heart was sinking.

In town they parted company. Kirk asked to be dropped at the fairgrounds near the rodeo arena so he could pay his entry fees. Beth watched him as he walked away, his bedroll thrown over his shoulder, his guitar case in hand. Too late, she remembered he'd asked to sleep in the truck. Why, then, did he take the bedroll with him? Of course he wouldn't want to leave it in an open pickup. He might have asked her to—No! She wasn't going to keep wondering whether he was going to disappear or not! She had a hard day's work to do.

But she was frightened, nevertheless. Had she done a very foolish thing, driving him here? Might she be held responsible if Kirk decided to bolt?

She checked into the lodge across the street, freshened up and drove to the auction barn.

Much of the livestock for tomorrow's sale had already been brought in; more would be arriving all day. Each animal had to be inspected, and most objected to the procedure. Today her assistant was a young cow-boy with ambitions of his own to become a brand in-spector. He was getting on-the-job training. They worked in the holding pens or, when necessary, in nar-row chutes. The cattle usually had to be roped and held in order for Beth to get a look at the brands, and often hair that had grown around the brand had to be cut away. The work was tiring because of the number of animals that had been trucked in for the sale. And it was dirty because the well-used holding pens were so dusty.

It was after seven o'clock when she returned to her motel. A warm bath eased her body, but the time spent by herself was not mentally relaxing. The opportunity to think only served to exhume the needling apprehen-sion—fear that Kirk had gone. The picture of him walking away, turning to give her a smile, was vivid in the forefront of her mind and wouldn't leave her.

Lying in the tub, head back, eyes closed, Beth tried to imagine how she would feel if she knew she'd never see him again. She'd feel like something deep inside was going to wither and die and leave a hollow space. Hol-low, because some part of her was taken away. He was so elusive—a dream that would turn to vapor if she ever tried to grab it. Beth pictured a leaf fallen from a tree, resting for some moments on the ground only to be caught by a passing gust of wind and swept away, far away, into a black forever.

Her eyelids shot open. In horror she stared at the white bathroom ceiling. "Oh, no!" she whispered. "Heaven help me, I'm in love with him!" The warm water that surrounded her suddenly felt hot, then cold and then hot again.

She called herself stupid. Called herself foolish. Called herself naive and silly and unbalanced and a myriad of names she'd never used before in her life. To Beth, the realization that she had fallen in love with a man so off-limits, so out of reach, meant only hurt. Deep and lasting hurt. She'd known someday she'd fall in love; it happened to almost everybody sometime. But she hadn't expected it to be now, not this way, and with nothing to come of it but pain.

Tonight's rodeo had already started. Kirk was supposed to be there; that is, if he was still in town. She had to know. And she wanted to see him ride. These few precious days before he was sent to prison would probably be all they'd ever have, even if Kirk wanted it otherwise. A criminal was definitely not what she had in mind for herself; she might be foolish but she wasn't insane.

She dressed in jeans and a white shirt and denim jacket, walked across the street to the rodeo grounds and bought a ticket. By the time she was seated in the stands, the bareback-bronc-riding event was underway. Halfway through the event the announcer called out Kirk's name; he was the next rider up. There was some hesitation, some confusion, and then the announcer's muffled voice could be heard saying to someone, "Where is he?" Shortly afterward a correction was made and another contestant's name was announced instead.

Beth sat numbed, unable to move. Kirk wasn't here! While another bronc came bouncing and jerking out of the chutes to the cheers of the crowd, she sat in a swirl of confusion, trying to make sense out of everything.

Why would Kirk sign up and pay entry fees if he wasn't going to stay? He had to have entered officially, because his name and the number he'd drawn were on tonight's lineup and hadn't been scratched.

For a time Beth lost hold of where she was. She didn't smell the dust of the arena or see it cloud in gusts under the spotlights at the pounding of hooves and the scraping of boot heels. She didn't hear the shouts of the cowboys below or the voices of the spectators around her. She didn't see the colors of the festival, except in a blur. What had Kirk done? What had *she* done by bringing him over here? She felt almost ill, and not so much for the fear that Kirk had jumped bail with her help as for the emptiness in her heart to think he might be gone from her life.

She watched the calf roping without really seeing any of it, not wanting to leave or be alone. In the beginning of the saddle-bronc-riding event, she was startled out of her reverie when she heard the announcer's voice boom, "Next out of chute number two, Kirk Hawthorne of Tumblecreek, Montana, on a horse called Halfway to Heaven!"

The gates opened within seconds, almost before Beth could react. She thrilled at seeing him ride. One arm in the air, he seemed to be hanging most of the time between his mount and the sky. It was easy to see how that horse had got its name. But she could tell the bronc wasn't going to give him a prizewinning ride, because in spite of Kirk's kicking, its bucking was too predictable.

He rode to the eight-second bell and slid off, making his way back across the arena without a glance in either direction. As Beth watched him, she thought, *he's a stranger to me*. As much as she had talked with him, she had no idea what he really thought about or what his goals in life were. This was the first time she'd ever heard the name of his hometown. He hadn't ever mentioned Tumblecreek and she had never heard of it.

He was the next-to-last contestant in the bull-riding contest, the last event of the evening. The bull he drew was spirited and mean, and he rode it like the champion he was, winning the applause of the audience.

The activity around the chutes thinned rapidly after the final ride. The contestants dispersed. Beth made her way to the front of the stadium, where she could see Kirk still hanging around, lending a hand with some of the livestock. Feeling almost light-headed from the relief of being wrong about his leaving Sioux Springs, she ran down the steps and hurried around the fence to the area back of the chutes. She climbed up onto the thick wood fence and waved at him; he was talking with another of the contestants. His number—twenty-six—was still pinned to the back of his light-blue shirt.

When he saw her he smiled. Quickly terminating his conversation, he walked toward her with the slow, easy strides she knew so well by now.

"You should be congratulated on that last ride," she said.

"Is that why you came down here?"

"Of course."

"I'm flattered as hell." He climbed up his side of the fence and over. "I'm a stranger in this town. What about you?"

"Almost."

"Good. With luck nobody will know us from any other traveling rodeo couple if you agree to have dinner with me. I've worked up a colossal appetite this afternoon."

"So have I, I realize, now that you mention appetites."

"They tell me there's a place a couple of blocks down the street where they have huge T-bones and tall beers."

"Sounds great." Beth smiled. "Turn around, Kirk."

"Huh?"

"Your number."

"Oh."

He turned and stood still while she unpinned it from his shirt, folded it and handed it to him. "Do you need this for tomorrow?"

"Yeah."

They began walking slowly. "You didn't even get your clothes dirty, Kirk. You managed to stay on your feet after both rides."

"Good thing, huh? This is one of the dustiest arenas I've ever seen. I'd hate to be in the company of a special lady looking like I'd been rolling in the dirt like a pig."

"Special lady?" Beth looked around playfully while her heart was responding with little skips. "Who might that be?"

"You know her," he said, taking her hand and squeezing it affectionately. "And I like getting to know her, more than anything I've ever done."

They walked around the curve of the arena toward the main office buildings. Beth asked, after a silence, "Where were you this afternoon?"

"What do you mean, where was I?"

"During the bareback-bronc riding. They announced your name and apparently couldn't find you. You must have had to forfeit your entry fee."

He didn't seem to want to look directly at her. "Yeah, I did . . . have to."

"I thought maybe something was wrong."

He shrugged. "I got delayed." Almost under his breath, he added by way of vague explanation, "Got involved in a poker game."

She sensed that he was lying. He didn't have that kind of money to throw away on rodeo fees nor did he likely have the kind of money it would take to gamble after he'd just paid all those fees. Whatever he'd been doing this afternoon, she doubted it was gambling at cards . . . although it could have been. What did she really know about how much money he had to spend? No, it was something else that made her feel he wasn't being truthful with her about his whereabouts. It was the manner in which he answered her—somehow different than he would have answered had he had nothing to hide.

They were adjacent to the arena office buildings now, where she had let him off this morning to sign up. The crowd had gone. The parking lot on the far side was empty. Only the dust was left, still visible under the floodlights that lit the entire area. Across the way, the lights in the small stadium had just been turned out. Silence lingered on echoes of the day's excitement and the night was turning colder. Kirk had not released her hand. He held it as they walked, fingers laced through hers, as if they had known each other for a long time and weren't virtual strangers.

There were no other people around except for a stout, tall man who was walking toward them. Lights went off in the low, one-story office building and a woman exited carrying a canvas envelope, obviously a money envelope.

The stout man was no sooner past them than they heard a scream. Turning swiftly in alarm, they saw that the woman had been knocked to the ground and the man was running toward the parking lot at full speed with the canvas bag.

Before she had a chance to fully comprehend what had happened, Kirk released her hand and took off in hot pursuit of the robber while the woman was screaming, "He has a knife!"

Kirk ignored the warning just as he ignored the fact that the other man had a very sure lead as he sped across the lot. Kirk was fast on his feet and he knew it; the distance began to close between them.

Beth knelt beside the injured woman, but her eyes were still fixed on the chase until the two men disappeared behind a building. Then, breathing almost as hard as if she had been running herself, she turned to the woman who was sitting up on the sidewalk, also watching the chase.

"How badly are you hurt?"

The woman rubbed her knee through her jeans. "I'm bruised a little, that's all." She struggled to her feet with Beth's assistance. "And shaking. That guy scared me to death! Damn him! That's the box-office proceeds he stole."

She was in her forties with gray-streaked red hair, and she was, Beth noted, shaking violently. Beth helped her back into the building. In less than two minutes Kirk had returned.

"I lost him," he panted.

"It's just as well," the woman said, "because if you'd caught him, he might have stabbed you. I...appreciate you trying, though."

"You'd better phone the police."

"Yes, I was just coming in here to get to a phone." Brightly painted nails trembled on the dial.

"I'll do it for you," Beth offered. "You'd better sit down."

Kirk stood in the open doorway, his chest heaving, looking out past the street lamps into the darkness. His fists were clenched. Beth watched him but gave most of her attention to helping the frightened woman.

A police car was just around the corner, half a minute away. Uniformed officers took separate descriptions of the thief from Beth and Kirk, who had gotten a look at his face when he passed them just before the attack. The description went out immediately on the police radio. They took a description of his knife from the victim and told all three there would probably be more questions at a later time.

Beth found it interesting that in identifying himself Kirk gave no mention of his present status with the police. Perhaps he felt it would complicate matters, even set himself up as a possible suspect—an accomplice or something. He was a rodeo contestant; that was all he felt they needed to know.

Afterward, at the restaurant, drinking beer, she asked him what she'd been wanting to ask for the past hour. "Kirk, why did you chase that thief tonight?"

Her question obviously caught him off guard, for he set down his glass abruptly, then picked it up again before he answered—with a question.

"What d'you mean, why?"

"You heard the woman say he was armed. If you had caught him you'd have been hurt. Why did you do it?"

"Because he deserved to be caught."

She gazed at him quizzically from across the table. He stared back. "What's with you, Beth?"

She shrugged self-consciously and took a swallow of beer. The ensuing silence was awkward.

He felt the need to bridge that silence. "You mean because I'm a thief myself, you're surprised I'd go to any risk or bother catching another thief. That's it, isn't it?"

This was the first time he had actually used the word in connection with himself. "Thief" sounded harsh and cold, and even though she was thinking it, to hear him say it was a jolt. She answered honestly, "Yes, something like that."

"It was—" he sipped again "—reflex action, that's all."

"Reflex?"

"Yeah, like a cat goes after anything that runs."

"Your pursuit was more like the reflex of a lawman than a . . . criminal . . . if you ask me."

He looked at her strangely while he rubbed the back of his neck as if it was stiff. "He knocked the woman to the ground," he said after a long pause. "Obviously hurt her. The guy is scum."

She recalled their first encounter by the windmill, when she'd known instinctively that Kirk wouldn't try to hurt her. There were many sides to this man, Beth realized, only a few of which she knew. His concern for this woman, his contempt for the thief and his disregard of personal danger at the time all added to her confusion. He was a combination of contradictions.

He walked back to the motel with her, holding her hand. "I hope you don't mind if I stashed my stuff in the cab of your pickup and locked the doors. I had it sitting at the office, but when I . . . later on this evening, when I saw your truck was parked at the motel and it wasn't locked, I took the liberty of using it. Is that okay?"

"Of course. I'd have suggested I keep your things for you myself, but I only thought of it after you left this morning."

They reached the motel parking lot, a small area filled to capacity. She took the keys from her handbag and unlocked the door of her pickup. Kirk reached in for his bedroll and guitar. He tossed the bedroll into the back of the truck and climbed up with the guitar case.

She stood watching him. "Do you sleep with your guitar?"

Kirk laughed. "I'm gonna strum awhile. Why not come on up?"

She accepted the offer of his outstretched hand. He untied the sleeping bag and unfolded it partway to give her a soft place to sit, close beside him.

The moon and stars were hidden by a cover of clouds that had moved in within the past two hours, so the night was very dark. The breeze was cool. She snuggled against the warmth of his body, thighs touching thighs, and listened to him softly play.

"This is how I relax," he said. "Best tranquilizer ever invented."

She was feeling far less relaxed, because of the nearness of him.

Soon he asked, "Are you cold?" and slid his arm around her. He looked down at her in the dim light of the motel's red neon sign, and she was certain he was about to kiss her when they heard voices addressing them.

"We've got beer," a man said. "Can we join you?"

Kirk seemed to recognize the cowboy. He was probably a rodeo contestant. "Sure," Kirk answered.

Two other couples, who had come from one of the motel rooms, climbed into the truck and introduced themselves. The men had all competed against Kirk that afternoon in saddle-bronc riding. They urged him to play, and everybody began to sing. When Beth finally left to go to bed, thinking about her busy day tomorrow, they were still out there drinking beer and singing. She wondered whether Kirk was going to get any sleep at all.

In the night she woke to the sound of rain against the window. Sleepily, she turned over, thinking what a lovely sound a summer night rain was—until the thought sank in and she sat up suddenly. Kirk! He would be soaked in the back of the pickup!

She rose and slipped into her clothes. Rain was falling softly but steadily. When she dashed for the truck, the raindrops felt like a thousand cold little stings against skin still warm from sleep.

He wasn't in the back. She opened the door. He was curled around the gearshift inside the cab, his guitar on the floor, his knees jammed against the dash. The overhead light roused him so quickly that she suspected he was just barely asleep, if he was asleep at all.

He raised his head and grunted, "It can't be morning yet."

"It's three in the morning. Did you get wet?"

"I'm okay. What are you doing out in the rain at this hour?"

"Worrying about you getting wet."

"Some downpour this is! But I'm starting to dry out."

"You look awfully uncomfortable."

"It wouldn't be so bad except for the gearshift. Next time get an automatic, will you?"

"Kirk, you can't possibly sleep like that. There are two beds in the room and I only need one of them. You'd better come inside."

He sat up. "You sure?"

"Of course I'm sure. This is ridiculous."

He began to gather up his bedroll. "You're getting soaked standing there."

"I know, I know...." She turned and hurried back across the narrow lot and entered her room again, leaving the door open behind her.

In seconds he was standing inside the room. "I feel like a stray dog."

"A stray *wet* dog," she said, looking him up and down in the light.

"Yeah. I was sound asleep and all of a sudden I found myself getting drenched. I made a dash for the cab. Tried not to get your seat too wet, though." He grinned. "You're almost as wet as I am, from trying to rescue me."

She grabbed a towel from the bathroom and rubbed her hair.

He set down the guitar. "As long as I'm here and no one happens to be in the shower..."

"Be my guest. It'll warm you up. You must be cold."

"I've been a lot colder." He began unbuttoning his shirt. "Sorry to disturb your sleep, Beth."

"It's no big deal."

"I appreciate this." He tossed the shirt on the bed that hadn't been slept in and went into the bathroom.

When she heard the shower running, Beth changed into her pajamas again, turned out the light and got into bed. She lay very still and very wide awake, listening to the rain on the window. Soon the sound of the shower ceased. Sudden light poured into the room when he opened the bathroom door. He quickly turned off the switch. Beth didn't open her eyes, but she was strongly aware of his presence, his every movement, as he padded across the room. She literally held her breath at the sound of the bedclothes being moved and then the squeaking of the springs as he settled into the bed.

At least five minutes later, his deep voice broke the dead silence of the room. "I can't sleep, either."

She was a long time in answering. "How did you know I wasn't sleeping?"

"These beds are...close."

"Yes...."

"My mother used to kiss me good-night on rainy nights like this, and then I could sleep. If I come over there, just for a minute, would you kiss me good-night?"

A wave of heat flowed through her at the memory of the devastating effects of his kiss. Her quickening heartbeat was all the proof she needed of how afraid she was of herself.

"Well?" he asked softly.

"Uh . . . are you . . . ? What are you . . . ?"

"What am I what?"

"Wearing?"

"Not a hell of a lot."

"Kirk, damn it, please just go to sleep. Please. You promised to be good."

"I did?"

"Well, sort of silently you did. You were being grateful."

"Oh. I guess I silently did promise to be good. Just one kiss, though? Just a good-night kiss. That's not so out of line, is it?"

She didn't answer. One part of her longed for the feel of his lips, the touch of his skin. But she was too afraid of what would happen to allow herself that luxury. These beds were too close together as it was! In the silence she could almost hear him breathing.

"Shorts," he said out of the darkness.

"What?"

"I'm wearing my undershorts. I swear I'm not naked."

This was the worst thing he could have said, because it made her remember how he looked when he was naked. Was he making her remember on purpose?

"Kirk . . ." Her voice was very unsteady.

"One little good-night kiss . . ." he repeated less playfully than before.

She heard the sheets move again. The room was so black she couldn't see a thing, but she felt his presence over her, and as he leaned closer, she could smell soap. His hands felt gently for her face. She felt his thumbs on her lips, sliding away so gently and his lips coming down to where his thumbs had been. His lips . . .

Beth reached up and touched him. All her fingers, widely spread, moved across his bare chest as he kissed her. At her touch he sighed within the kiss. He knelt on the floor beside her bed and encircled her with his arms, never moving his lips away from hers, kissing her harder with each thundering second. Beth scarcely recognized the deep, throaty groan she heard through the darkness as her own.

8

IT WAS HE who reluctantly ended the kiss. Beth felt chilled when he moved the warmth of his body away. She wanted to plead with him to stay and, at the same time, to thank him for not doing so. The helplessness was overwhelming—helplessness from emotions too powerful to comprehend, much less control.

The darkness somehow made it worse. She couldn't see his eyes, but she knew they had been closed when he kissed her. She couldn't see his lips when they moved from hers, nor his chest, but she could feel his chest heaving. She couldn't see his body, yet she knew his body wanted her. The darkness held no secrets back.

"Beth...." he murmured, caressing her hair. "Good night...."

Her response was merely a whisper, and an effort even then. "Good night."

WHEN SHE WOKE, Kirk was still sleeping soundly. She lay for a time watching him. He was sprawled on his stomach, his face turned toward her, his hair in his eyes and his arms curved above his head. He was so perfect, so masculine; even his world was exclusively male.

Beautiful women frightened him, he'd told her. Beth had the feeling he didn't really know much about women, except through instinct. He was deeply aware of a woman's physical fragility in comparison to his own strength. He seemed to have no problem accepting her profession of brand inspector, which was usually considered a man's profession, and he admired her skills on horseback. He accepted her as a person, yet he never forgot for an instant that she was a woman; his eyes told her that. There was something, though, some intuitive feeling that made her think he *was* afraid of something to do with her.

If he ever came anywhere close to looking vulnerable, he did so in sleep. His strange past, of which he spoke so little, his secrets, the bleakness of his immediate future—none of this disturbed his sleep. He slept deeply, not moving except for the flicker of an eyelid and the slight twitching of his fingers. He slept like a little boy after a hard day of play.

Even when she moved, he didn't stir. Beth gathered her clothes, showered and dressed in the bathroom, and when she came out into the room again he was still sleeping. He was in almost the same position, except that one bare leg and foot were out of the covers. Beth smiled, blew him a silent kiss and closed the door quietly behind her when she left.

Concentrating on work today was going to be more difficult than usual, Beth reflected as she drove to the auction barn. But she'd have to get into it, because it would be about as busy as a day could get. Coffee and a little breakfast at the auction coffee shop would help. The sale itself began at two in the afternoon. Before then, she'd have to make certain the brand of every animal had been inspected. She looked at her watch. Six o'clock. She should have been up and out of the room an hour ago.

IT WAS ALMOST SEVEN O'CLOCK by the time she returned to the motel that evening. The beds were made. Except for his sleeping bag, rolled neatly in a corner, and his guitar, there was no sign that Kirk had ever been there. Beth showered and changed and, just as she had done last night, walked across the street to the fairgrounds stadium. The sky was cloudy, but there was no sign of rain tonight, at least not yet.

Last night's rain had served to eliminate some of the rodeo dust, but the sandy soil had dried in the sunshine of the day, so there was no mud. Kirk rode a bareback bronc and a bull, and as usual, his rides looked sensational from the stands. Staying on a bucking bronc looked like far less effort when Kirk was doing it than when most of the other contestants took the challenge. Getting off the bronc, he fell and didn't get up for several seconds. Beth leaned forward in her seat with shortened breath and a pang of fear, but he got to his feet without assistance, favoring one leg slightly.

He must have taken a million spills, she thought. Broken a lot of bones. It was part of the sport. Why did they call it a sport, anyhow? Kirk did it for money, not because it was fun. Didn't he?

It seemed natural meeting him behind the chutes after the rodeo, as she'd done the night before. He had expected her to be there. They had dinner together in a place she'd heard about in the afternoon, a steak house on the opposite side of town far enough away for them

to succeed in dodging the two couples they'd met last
night at the hotel. Nothing was said out loud about
their wanting the chance to be alone tonight, but the
electricity of last night was still with them, tensing the
very air around them. Closeness in the dark of night.
A kiss in the dark of night that was not a kiss between
strangers.

When they were driving back to the motel after dinner, Kirk said, "It isn't raining tonight."

"Not now, but it may."

"Yeah, it may. One never knows."

"I really don't think," she said slowly, "that you ought
to take that chance—of rain."

"You don't?" His voice lowered after a poignant
pause. "You're sure, Beth?"

"I'm sure. Anyway, your guitar is in the room."

"You prefer a more private party tonight?"

She merely looked at him.

And he answered her silence. "So would I."

Inside the motel room, Beth switched on the lamp
between the beds and turned to him. "You're still favoring your right leg. That was a bad spill you took
getting off the bronc. Are you okay?"

"Just bruised. An occasional limp is a requirement
of the profession."

Rubbing his thigh just above the knee, Kirk sat down
on the bed, kicked off his boots, unbuckled his belt and
unbuttoned his jeans.

"What are you doing?"

"Checking my wounds. You don't mind, do you? I
mean, it isn't as if you haven't seen me with my pants
off before."

Her breath caught on a sigh. He knew the churnings within her; he couldn't help but know. He'd always known. "Why do you keep reminding me every chance you get?"

"Do I?"

"You know you do."

He smiled. "Maybe because you're so pretty when you blush."

"I don't like to blush."

"I know. Okay, I'll be good and stop teasing you." This he said while proceeding to remove his jeans, pulling them gingerly over the right knee and wincing slightly.

Trying to give her full attention to his leg, none to his dark-blue shorts, Beth sat on the bed beside him. "It is badly bruised."

"Nah. Not that bad. A hot shower and I'll be fine. Okay if I take a shower in your bathroom?"

"If you're stiff from the fall, maybe a soak in a hot tub would help more."

"A bath?" He said it as if he barely understood the word. "I've never soaked in a hot tub in my life. I wouldn't know how."

"No. . . ." She looked at him, smiling thoughtfully. "I suppose you wouldn't."

He was unbuttoning his shirt. Tossing it onto the bed, he walked to the bathroom wearing only the brief undershorts. "I won't be long."

"Take your time."

He did. The shower ran for a long time, while she moved restlessly around the room. She turned on the radio. The soft music seemed to seep out through dusty memories of long-ago days and long-ago dreams, of girlhood emotions, girlhood dreams, almost forgotten. Romantic dreams about falling in love someday with the perfect man, her prince. When she closed her eyes the sight of Kirk in the brief shorts was as clear as if he was still standing there. His body was so perfect. Husky arms and legs, broad shoulders, a flat stomach. She moaned and thought, *what have I gotten myself into?*

Kirk was thinking almost the same thing. Standing in the shower, letting the hot water wash over his body and splash in his face, he tried to come to terms with his raging emotions. Never had he thought so much about a woman as he thought of Beth—during moments of the day and night when he didn't expect the thoughts of her to come, they did. And they stayed, pushing everything else from his mind for minutes at a time. Never had he been so fascinated by a woman. Never had he wanted a woman the way he wanted her.

And the feelings were mutual; he was sure of it. In spite of believing he was a criminal and being hesitant about getting too involved with him, Beth wanted him as much as he wanted her. She wasn't good at pretending, and she'd admitted she didn't even try. It was one of the things he loved about her—she was totally honest. If only the same were true of him, he thought. When Beth found out he had lied to her about his identity, she'd have every right to be furious. She wouldn't like being lied to. Hell, *he* wouldn't want to be lied to, either. It was a touchy situation, and he didn't like it at all, but he couldn't change it.

Nor could he deny his feelings, as he'd intended to do, for her sake. He'd felt the warmth and softness of her body last night, in the dark, and it had taken every bit of self-discipline he could muster to release her. The way she had responded to his kiss had left him too restless to sleep. She wanted him as much as he wanted her. Her eyes had said so. Her body warm against his had said so. And her lips . . . her lips had said so. . . . He was beginning to feel certain that her heart wanted him, too, responding to the beats of his own heart. It was impossible for him to deny any longer that he was falling in love with her.

When he returned to the bedroom with a towel wrapped around his waist, Beth was sitting on the bed, barefoot, propped against pillows, listening to the radio. In the soft light, the delicate shadows of her eyelashes on her cheek symbolized to him her fragile, feminine beauty.

He was vigorously drying his hair. She looked up at him with a strange expression for an instant, as though she was seeing him for the first time, and then a mistiness clouded her eyes. She seemed to be reading his mind.

He smiled. "You look lovely."

"So do you. Wet and wild."

He sat down on the edge of the bed and leaned over to kiss her gently on the cheek, then on the lips. Beth trembled against his bare chest, too aware that he was nearly naked, too aware of his eyes and what she had seen in them, in the reflection of herself. Her trembling was almost uncontrollable, and feeling it, he held her tight.

She breathed his name on a shaky breath. He responded by brushing back her hair and gazing deeply into her eyes. His voice came in a husky whisper. "Don't be afraid of me, Beth. You've nothing to fear from me."

She felt like crying. "Yes...I have. I fear that..." She couldn't say it.

"What? What could you fear?"

"Only that you'll . . . disappear . . . suddenly just . . . disappear."

"I won't disappear."

"Perhaps you won't have that choice to make. You'll have to leave."

Kirk was silent for some moments. The music of the radio was the only sound around them. He answered at last, "I won't leave, Beth. I promise."

"How can you promise?"

"I do promise, that's all." He was caressing her hair.

She tried to keep control of herself, of the situation, but it was hard with him sitting there without anything on but a towel. "I want to take a . . . shower."

"Okay." He moved aside and put out a hand to help her up.

When she came out of the bathroom some twenty minutes later, wearing her pink satin robe, Kirk was not in the room. His bedroll was there in the corner with his guitar, and his shirt lay on the bed where he had tossed it earlier, but his jeans and his jacket and his boots were gone. And so was he.

Beth didn't have long to puzzle about it. Within five minutes she heard the key in the lock and he came in carrying a paper bag.

"I walked over to the store and decided to pick up some champagne." He paused and stared at her. "You're beautiful in pink satin. Do we have two glasses?"

"Champagne? Oh . . . sure. I'll get them."

The paper of the bag crinkled as he took out the bottle. "I had to get something that didn't require a corkscrew. I don't generally carry one on my person." He began to work at the safety wire. "Do you like champagne?"

"I love champagne."

"So do I. But I don't advertise the fact to my beer-guzzling buddies."

He unzipped his jacket and threw it over a chair. Bare chested, he proceeded to pour the champagne, then handed one of the sparkling glasses to her.

The bubbles tickled her tongue and the roof of her mouth. "Are we celebrating?"

"Yeah."

"What?"

"Us. Our meeting and our—" He took another drink. "We're celebrating the night—this night." He held up his glass. "To us."

There was no mistaking, positively no mistaking, what Kirk meant. It had all come about so naturally somehow. It seemed so . . . right. It wasn't supposed to seem right, but it did.

The whole world had become this room. They were isolated here just as they'd been isolated in the hills the day he'd first kissed her. What his life was—out there—didn't matter here in this room, on this night. Here they were only a man and a woman overmastered by the powerful forces of love. Beth's early doubts had been held by a dam of sticks, easily washed away by the persuasion of Kirk's eyes and the wakening needs within her.

The dam of doubt was broken, and he knew it.

He set down his glass. Circling her in his arms, he kissed her, running his hands over her robe. "Satin and champagne," he whispered. "Both so . . . soft. . . ."

"You like softness?"

"I'm not used to anything soft . . . like this . . . like you. . . ." His lips were touching her temple. "But yes . . . I like softness. . . ."

From behind another silence, his lips touching her cheek, her neck, he murmured, "Is your skin as soft as this satin?"

"It couldn't be. . . ."

"I think it could."

"Then touch me and see. . . ."

Gingerly he slid the fabric from her shoulders, kissing her skin, rubbing his cheek over her shoulder. "Umm . . . yes . . . even softer. . . ."

She felt him tremble.

"Kirk . . . I feel so strange. . . ."

He didn't lift his head. He was kissing her shoulder. "Bad strange or good strange?"

She smiled softly. "Good strange."

"So do I."

Yielding to his kisses and to his hands, now sliding pink satin down from over her breasts, she muttered into his chest, "I feel like my whole body is a pool of champagne bubbles."

"Do *I* make you feel like champagne bubbles?"

"Yes."

His lips trailed over her breasts like a brush of fire. She breathed his name again and again.

He whispered, "Beth . . . honey . . . are you sure?"

She could only nod now; tears of emotion glazed her eyes. Tangled too far in the web of her need to think of consequences, Beth felt herself being lifted by gentle arms, felt the bed under her and Kirk over her, covering her. Her robe parted and fell away from her thighs.

When she squirmed slightly at the cold contact of his belt buckle, Kirk stood and unfastened the belt. His eyes remained on her.

"You're so beautiful, Beth. I can't keep from wanting you. I've . . . I've wanted you. . . . I'm only a man with the feelings of a man, and I couldn't talk myself out of wanting you."

"Did you try?"

"I did try. But not for my sake. For yours."

She watched as he undid his jeans, watched as he stepped out of them. They fell, crumpling the paper bag that had held the champagne. As if the crackling sack reminded him, Kirk reached for their unfinished glasses. Beth sat up and accepted the glass from him.

They drank for a moment or two in silence, until she said softly, "I tried, too. I didn't want to want you. It seemed so out of sync with everything in my life, and it seemed so . . . kind of hopeless."

It took Kirk a moment to understand. He tended to forget he was in a masquerade. He answered, "It isn't hopeless, though."

"What isn't?"

"Us."

She sighed shakily and handed him back the glass. "Kirk, make me forget. Make me forget everything...."

"I will... I promise...." He leaned forward, kissing her again, softly at first, then more deeply, and deeper still, until she moaned. His hands fumbled over the satin belt of her robe, and when the robe fell free, he caressed her thighs as he kissed her. Beth felt the sensation of her body going light, almost weightless, as if she could float into his body and be a part of him. And he, in his way, was pulling her into his body, into his soul. Into his life.

Her hands moved over the expanse of his shoulders, down over his back, fingers fluttering one moment and grasping hard the next, holding him close to her. When she reached the band of his bikini shorts, he shifted to allow her to slide them away.

There was music from the radio, barely heard. It wafted up and over them and blended warmly with the shadows of the room. A trembling sigh overtook her; she hardly knew whether it was hers or his. Heartbeats thundering—hers or his? Both together.

Kirk's lips came gently over hers, gently moving, gently sighing. Over her neck. Over her breasts, warm in his hands. Surrender was so easy; she floated there on a cloud of down... accepting.

Accepting fire-edged kisses over her body, powdery sparkles of heat all over, Beth lay still until she had to move. She laced her fingers through his thick hair, then found his neck and his solid shoulders. Hands on his chest, moving against the dark curls of hair. Hands on his waist, his hips, while he explored the mysteries of her body with his lips.

He blew softly on her and the warmth of his breath sent shivers of passion through her.

"Kirk..."

"Tell me what you like," he whispered.

"You already know...."

He moved down and she felt his breath again, and soon his arms about her waist. He whispered, "Bear with me, Beth, this time. You excite me so much I'm not going to last.... I can't help it."

"I want to excite you that much...." Her voice came on barely audible sighs.

"Honey, is it all right? Are you all right?"

The question sank in slowly and hit with a pang of panic. "Oh! No! Kirk, it's not all right! I didn't... think...."

Her body went to battle with her mind. Passion wilder than any she had ever known ensnared her, bewitched her, burned her, while her conscious mind suddenly found cause to fight. She hadn't even thought... Tears jumped to the surface of her eyes.

His voice came half mumbled, half whispered. "It's all right. I have something."

"You what? Kirk, I can't believe you carry...."

Two fingers fell gently on her lips to hush her. "Of course I don't. I told you, I went to the store." He replaced his fingers on her mouth with his lips, kissing her deeply, while she could hear him rattle the sack beside the bed. "I hate this interruption," he whispered, "but it can't be helped."

And she could only mutter, "I know," with a deep sense of gratitude that protecting her mattered to him, that he had told the truth when he'd said he would never hurt her.

The warmth of his body did not leave her. Beth closed her eyes, languishing in the warmth of him in the song that was their love. She floated out on the pillowy cloud again, losing herself in her desire for him, desire turning to an ache of growing anticipation to be nearer and nearer still—to become a part of him.

And he was there, his body hard and solid and warm above her, his lips and tongue bathing her with splashes of kisses again, his hands caressing more boldly than before.

He whispered her name on the strains of the soft music in the room, and she answered only, "Yes," feeling her heart soar with the joy of a moment that would live with her forever.

She moaned. So did he. She grasped his shoulders tightly, trying to keep a hold on something solid. There seemed to be a night sky formed around them, moonlit, full of darting stars. Space, endless space. But no earth. She could not hold on to the spinning planet anymore, and soon she ceased to try.

Kirk was her reality; there was no other. And she was one with him now.

The warmth and acquiescence of her was to Kirk like some long and close-held memory returning. But it was not a memory; it was instead a dream. Because there was no memory; no one like her had ever been in his life. The dream had existed, though—the dream of a woman's softness unlike any other, of a woman's complete surrender to him. The dream of a special kind of love, unknown to his heart until today.

Passion built on love until he could barely tell where they merged. Her body found the rhythm of his, her breaths the rhythm of his; her heart, too, beat in the rhythm of his. Faster . . . harder. Until the stars of the night sky seemed to find voices and begin to sing.

9

SHE FELT THE BED SAG under his weight when he came back from the bathroom. His fingers caressed her hair and she opened her eyes. He seemed very far away at first, gazing down at her, and his voice seemed faraway, but slowly it came closer.

He asked, "Are you all right?"

She nodded and smiled up at him. "Are you?"

Her response made him chuckle softly. "I'm drained and limp and sapped of strength and I've never felt better in my life." Absently, he twirled a lock of her hair and repeated, "Never."

"Me, either."

"You're very special, Beth. I've known it from the first moment I saw you."

"When you first saw me you were mad at me."

"And you were afraid of me."

"Yes."

"Are you still afraid?"

"Do I look afraid?"

He smiled. "No, only beautiful. I just can't believe how beautiful, even more than before...before tonight."

"Tonight has changed me."

His voice was husky. "It's changed me, too."

"In what way?"

Kirk hesitated. He couldn't tell her how he wanted her in every way there was to want a woman. He wanted her to be with him, be part of him and of his life. He had suspected it before he'd made love to her, but now he knew for sure she was the best thing that had ever happened to him. She was a woman to make him forget the past and to dream of a future.

But he couldn't tell her so. A thief awaiting trial couldn't tell her, because he had no right to. The drifter who only yesterday was moving rustled cattle for pay couldn't tell her, because he had no right to. And the sheriff's deputy working undercover to catch a mob of cattle thieves couldn't tell her, either.

He had no right to confuse her. No right to stain her reputation because of what she and everyone else believed him to be. And most of all he had no right to endanger her. The possibility loomed very real that somewhere along the line his cover could be blown. A face in a crowd—the rodeo crowd, perhaps—who recognized him. A slipup when he was following Marty. From experience he knew only too well that these things could happen. He was dealing with criminals—he was engaged in double-crossing criminals! And that could be dangerous, not only for him but for anyone who might be close to him. It was better to lie to Beth than to endanger her.

That still didn't make it easy. She lay looking up at him now, her chestnut hair flowing onto the white pillow, and waiting for his answer. How had tonight changed him? About that, he couldn't lie to her. His answer came so huskily he had to clear his throat. "I'll never stop wanting you . . . now that I know what it's like to make love with you."

She looked at him sadly. "Never is a long time."

"Yeah. . . ."

"What's going to happen, Kirk?"

"I don't know, honey. Let's not think about anything now. . . . Sometimes we have to live just for the day. Can you do that?"

"I always try to do that, but—"

"Good." He kissed her. "So do I."

Under the blanket his hand began to move in gentle circles over her thigh. He lay in silence for a time, caressing her tenderly.

"Beth?"

"Hmm?"

"We can't be seen together."

"I don't think it would bother me all that much to be seen with you."

"It would bother me. And I'm sure it would bother your family."

"Yes, I guess my family would have a major adjustment to make if we were seen together around Prairie Hills, especially if we were seen as lovers."

"I don't want to put you through that. I just won't do it. It isn't fair."

"I can decide for myself what I choose to go through or not go through. I'm stronger than I look."

He smiled. "I know you are. But you also have a lot of common sense. Beth, there's just no reason why anyone should have to know about us. It's no one's business but ours, is it?"

"No, it's no one else's business. And it *would* start an avalanche of gossip."

"Who needs the world?" He smiled, still moving his hand sensually over her skin.

"Right. Who does?"

Gossip wouldn't hurt this man in the least, Beth realized. He was doing all this insisting for her sake. And she loved him all the more for it.

He had promised not to leave her, but that promise wasn't up to him to keep. Beth had lied when she'd told him she lived for today, because the future haunted her. The picture in her mind of Kirk behind bars haunted her, just as the memory of the handcuffs did. How could he not leave her if they sent him to prison? As she lay in his arms, she closed her eyes and dared to ask him what she hadn't ever dared before. "Kirk?"

"Hmm?"

"What do they want to send you to prison for? What are the charges against you?"

When his body tensed, Beth almost wished she hadn't asked. But she wanted to know.

"Theft."

"Theft of what?"

"Just..." He sighed. "I really don't want to talk about it right now."

"Neither do I, but I can't help being curious. Wouldn't you be, if you were me?"

"Yeah, I guess so. Look, someday I'll tell you all about it, I promise. But I'm not..." His voice trailed off. He couldn't say any more. No more lies, because he hated them; no truth, because he didn't dare. Not when anyone Beth might know, anyone she might talk to, could be the man he was looking for. One hint from her that he was not who he pretended to be and it could be all over. The man whom Marty—and he—were working for might become suspicious.

"Not what?" she urged. "You're not what?"

"Not in the mood to talk," he mumbled apologetically.

"You sound tired. Are you sleepy?"

"Lord, no! Are you kidding? With you lying next to me all warm and naked . . . and rendering me hot and helpless?"

"Hot, maybe. I don't know about the helpless."

"I'm getting more helpless by the moment. Wanting you again . . ."

"So soon?"

He turned onto his back. "If you touch me, I'll be helpless. I'll be completely under your spell."

The fluttering deep inside her intensified. She turned on her side, facing him. "If I. . . ."

"Touch me, Beth . . . touch me. . . ."

She moved her hand slowly, teasingly, over his chest and his abdomen, in circles that became smaller, traveled lower, until Kirk moaned. He writhed and kicked away the sheet that covered them.

"Don't stop. . . ."

Lamplight shone softly on his suntanned body. There was a deep line where the tan stopped. Wherever he'd spent the summer, he must have been swimming often, and not in the nude, except when she'd seen him. Her shyness ebbed with the spontaneity of surging desire. She, too, was learning things she'd never known about helplessness. And strength.

If only for the moment, she possessed this man. She held him captive to his ripened passion. At his invitation, she could possess him completely. This night. Now.

"Kiss me..." he whispered on an exhaling breath, lying back on the pillow, his eyes closed.

Trembling, she leaned over and kissed his eyes and then his mouth, softly. He returned the kiss, holding her.

Then he whispered, "I meant...."

"I know what you meant."

"Will you?"

"Yes...."

He released his arms from around her.

"Close your eyes..." she whispered.

Music surrounded them. He didn't know how much of the music was real and how much was manufactured in his brain because of the spell she was casting upon him. His fingers tangled in her hair. His thighs trembled. His breath caught in his throat when he tried to say, "Don't stop," but he didn't have to say it. She knew. Oh, how she knew!

His body fought to release the unbearable tension soaring and diving within him. He fought so, writhed so, tearing at the sheets, that Beth became alarmed.

"No...don't stop..." he pleaded. "Don't let me go...."

She stayed with him until his groan filled the quiet of the room, and even longer, until he lay still again.

His arms came around her and he held her for a long time. She lay against his chest, feeling his heartbeat gradually return to normal. It was good in his arms. Beth had never felt she belonged anywhere more than she belonged here. The last words he had spoken—minutes ago now—were still reverberating in her ears. *"Don't let me go."* She hadn't then; she wouldn't now. Not if she could help it. Unless he chose to leave her or unless forces more powerful than both of them took Kirk away from her, she'd never let him go! She loved him.

Eventually he stirred. "I'm thirsty. Are you?"

"I'd love some more champagne. But who's going to move to get it?"

"I will. A few minutes ago I thought I'd never move again, thanks to you, but suddenly the thought of champagne motivates."

When he moved away from her she felt suddenly colder, the same way she had the first time he'd kissed her, only more so. They'd been two strangers then. Now they were lovers. Now they were part of each other.

He rolled from the bed and found the bottle and the glasses and poured them full. Turning back to her, he winced. "This bed is an indescribable mess! Who did this?"

"You did."

"Me? I did?"

"You don't remember?"

"No. . . ."

She looked at him over the rim of her glass. "You're very noisy, too."

"Am I? I didn't know that, either. It must be you—what you do to me."

She smiled. "That's right. Blame me."

He smiled back. "I love what you do to me. But I didn't mean to tear the bed to pieces." He made a clumsy attempt at straightening the sheet. "Are you tired?"

She shook her head. "But you need some rest. You have a rodeo tomorrow."

"That's no big deal."

"You love it, don't you? Riding those mean, dangerous animals?"

"I like the money."

"I think it's more than that or you wouldn't do it."

"You're right," he admitted. "I like the challenge."

"And the danger."

"Yeah, maybe."

"It's easy, isn't it? Easy for you, I mean—staying on a bucking bronc?"

"Yeah." He rubbed the back of his neck and grinned like a little boy.

Beth settled back on the rumpled sheets, pulled a corner of the top sheet loosely over her, tucked a pillow at her back and sipped her champagne. "Kirk, do you know how to play any lullabies?"

"You want a lullaby?"

"Would you?"

He set down his glass and rose to get his guitar. Still naked, he sat on the bed and strummed awhile, tuning the strings. "I wrote a song for you," he said, looking at the guitar strings and not at her. He hummed the gentle tune for a moment, then began to sing a ballad that brought tears to her eyes.

"You gathered dust from an open road
In the soft blue gaze of twilight

And made a path for me to walk
In the moon of midnight.

"You took the breath from evening wind
Sighs from the blowing rains
And made a love song from the sounds
Of lonely windswept plains."

Kirk sang the last line a second time, in a voice so soft she could barely hear it, as if it came from his heart and not from his throat.

Beth could scarcely hold back the tears as he continued to strum softly. How poignantly painful his song was—heart wrenching, like a goodbye.

"It wasn't meant to make you cry."

"I know. I'm not crying."

He lay the guitar aside and kissed the tear that stained her cheek. When he pulled away, in the lamplight she could see more distinctly than ever the shadows in his eyes.

ON MONDAY MORNING, after Theo had left the breakfast table and they heard his truck leaving the yard, Beth lingered with her stepmother over coffee. Lila was a woman, too, Beth thought, and surely she had experienced being in love. Lila and Beth's father must have been in love. The two of them had seemed so happy together, especially in the earliest months of their marriage. Lila had also come from somewhere else, out of a rather mysterious past. She and her father had met through friends in Denver when her father had been there on a business trip. Lila rarely mentioned her first husband, Theo's father, or her life before she came to Prairie Hills and the Circle C Ranch.

"You look especially lovely this morning, Beth," her stepmother said, pouring more coffee for them both. "Have you changed your makeup?"

"No."

"Well, something about you seems different. What is it?"

Beth shrugged and sipped her coffee innocently.

"Could it be a man, by any chance? You stayed a day longer in Sioux Springs than you'd planned."

"Why would you think it's a man?"

Lila smiled. "I haven't much imagination, dear, as you know. I can't think what else besides some special man could make your eyes shine so."

Beth laughed. "You're always hoping, aren't you, Lila?"

"That you'll meet someone wonderful and fall in love? Of course! That's what life is all about. Was there a rodeo dance in Sioux Springs?"

"I don't think so. I haven't danced with any man since—" she looked at the other woman carefully "—since Kirk Hawthorne."

"Kirk Hawthorne! Good heavens, Beth, surely you aren't still thinking about that . . . that . . ." Her voice seemed to fail her; she merely blinked.

"I do think about him, yes."

Lila's hand went to her throat, fingers spread. "Why?"

"He's very . . . nice."

"He's a common criminal!"

"I know."

"Don't be taken in by a man like that, darling. I've heard about him—heard he's very handsome and dripping with charm. That's just the type, Beth, just the type that's the most dangerous. He's tried to see you, hasn't he?"

Beth sipped, holding her cup in both hands, her elbows on the table, trying to look casual.

"I knew it! It's the Circle C he's after! He'll try whatever he can to get you to fall for him!"

Struggling to keep her voice calm, Beth said, "He's probably going to prison, Lila, maybe for a long time, so I don't think you have to worry."

China clinked against the saucer as Lila set down her cup. "Yes, I heard that he was going to trial here in Prairie Hills, but no one knows when."

Beth shrugged. Her heart was aching. She loved him, but she couldn't set her mind to wait for him to get out of prison. No, she wouldn't live that way! His crimes were more than he wanted to let on; they had to be. Every indication, from the handcuffs to his evasive answers, led to the obvious conclusion that his crimes were serious. She knew now that she didn't want to know what Kirk had done; she wanted to hold on to her dream, no matter how temporary it was. However short-lived, the dream was more beautiful than anything she had ever known.

"Every woman is vulnerable," Lila was saying gently, "to the charms of a man like Kirk Hawthorne. I saw him one day in town when Theo pointed him out to me. I thought to myself, oh, yes, now I understand! Women's heads were turning when he walked out of the post office." Lila smiled almost dreamily at the memory and sighed. "Oh, yes, I understand. I was young once, too. But be warned, Beth. Please be warned. I know what I'm talking about when I say you'll only be hurt if you have any more to do with that man." Her nose wrinkled and her voice hardened. "That thief."

Beth swallowed. Lila could be so convincing. She thought of the secrets that lurked in Kirk's silver-blue eyes. "Well," she said lamely, "like I said, he's going to prison, so he won't be around here for long, anyhow."

"I hope so. I'm sure prison's the right place for the likes of him. At least you'll be safer."

Beth drained her cup. The newspaper was on the table beside her, but she hadn't bothered to read anything except the headlines. Now her eyes happened to focus on the date. The twenty-first! Today was the twenty-first! Theo's telephone conversation, every detail of it, spun through her mind.

She looked up. "Lila, where did Theo go this morning?"

"He didn't say. Why?"

"He seemed in a rush."

"Theo is always in a rush. Did you ever see him when he wasn't?"

"I guess not."

"It's Monday. Are you taking the day off, Beth, or are you going to work?"

"I'm going to work for a while, and I'd better get moving." She pushed her chair back from the table. "See you tonight, Lila."

BETH AND KIRK had planned to meet in the hills in the late afternoon. Just for a little while, they'd decided, just to see each other. He didn't show up and Beth was alarmed. The ranch was less than a mile's ride, and Tom didn't keep an eye on Kirk; surely he'd had no problem getting away from his job. His puzzling breach of promise reminded her of the afternoon he'd failed to make an appearance at the rodeo in Sioux Springs after having paid his fees to ride. There'd been no apparent reason for his absence then, either, and his excuse hadn't been a truthful one, she was sure. Kirk was hiding something, and given what she knew of him, it was quite possibly something illegal.

A few hours later an evening news report had the entire valley in an uproar. A theft of forty head of Herefords had occurred at a large ranch in a neighboring county. Most of the stolen cattle weren't branded, the television newscaster reported. They'd been taken from a single pasture where fresh track marks from a large truck had been discovered at around noon today—July twenty-first.

The news stunned Beth, stunned them all. It was the main conversation at their dinner table that night, as it must have been in every home in the area. Remembering Theo's strange telephone conversation, Beth was plagued by grim discomfort. The rustled cattle had not yet been branded. It was implied the thieves had been aware of that fact, which could also imply they knew when the branding was to be. As before, the calves had been loaded into a large vehicle believed to be a flatbed truck. And they had been taken in the early-morning hours. Surely, she thought, it was just a weird coincidence that this had happened on the twenty-first. Theo was a busy man with all kinds of business transactions going on all the time; it was just a coincidence this rustling happened on the date she'd overheard.

And Kirk? The first uneasy flutter of trepidation heightened to a near spasm when she forced her thoughts to him. *Where had Kirk been today?* Was his absence a coincidence, too?

Feeling slightly shaky, Beth excused herself and went out into the fresh air of the summer night, to the sanctuary of the meadow. The other day—the day of the rodeo, when he'd said he was playing cards—there had been a rustling incident the night before, farther north, in Cherry County.

No! she scolded herself. She was catching the paranoia that this cattle rustling had brought down on the valley.

Theo had acted perfectly normally tonight, eating heartily as always. Yet under her intense scrutiny, he had seemed slightly more subdued than usual, slightly less talkative. But why wouldn't he be? Everybody was. Every time there was another cattle theft they had to wonder who was going to be hit next. Theo, like everybody else, was worried about his herd. Beth was worried, too. But she found herself in the dismal state of worrying less about her cattle than about her gut-felt suspicions. Theo's damn phone call. Kirk's unexplained absences.

Crickets chirped in a loud chorus and frogs croaked as she walked along a meadow path with the big mongrel dog, James, at her side. Theo's phone conversation wouldn't be forgotten. Beth shuddered. She didn't believe suspicion this flimsy herself. There was just a nagging feeling that refused to let her go. Something was needling her deep inside.

She looked back at the huge house. Light was glowing from most of the windows on the ground floor—Theo's and Lila's floor. The rooms she used upstairs were dark—the room that was her father's, and long ago her mother's and father's together. She could barely remember those early days, except for a memory of her mother in the bed, pale and ill and smiling with her lips while her eyes were moist with tears. So long ago. Now the room was as her father had left it, unused except by guests. Lila slept in the remodeled bedroom downstairs across the hall from Theo. Dark, too, now in the middle hours of evening was the room where Beth had slept as a child. She slept there still, with mementos of her life all around her: her stuffed teddy bear, ribbons from horse shows, trophies from rodeo barrel races, old photos, even empty perfume bottles she should have thrown out and never had because the lingering scent reminded her of some special day, some special time.

It felt so frightening all of a sudden—the dark of the upstairs rooms, Theo's mother downstairs and the scary little feeling inside her when she'd looked at her stepbrother across the table tonight. Something was wrong. And then there were the ugly, niggling thoughts about Kirk, who was, after all, a criminal.

Wasn't she being ridiculous? Beth gritted her teeth in the solitude of the night. Theo was so good to her, had always been—Theo and Lila, both. It was just restlessness, she decided. Just missing her father, who had always been an anchor for her on nights like this when she was riddled with confusion. It was the heartache of being in love and wanting Kirk to cling to and whisper her doubts to, wanting to shout her love to the stars and the moon but knowing it was wrong, wrong, wrong, because Kirk was going to leave her. His promise was a summer wind, warm and soft, and then . . . gone. His promises, like his promise to be in the hills today, were lighter than the wind.

It was the despair of a hopeless love that was bothering her most tonight, more than she wanted to admit. The big house—her house—blazing with light, the news broadcast and her own overactive imagination . . . Everything was bothering her. Were the shadows in Kirk's eyes a product of her imagination? Was Theo's subtle preoccupation at dinner imagined, too? It was, she told herself. It was! Nevertheless, she made a determined decision. Tomorrow, when Theo was out, she'd have a look around his office.

EVERYTHING IN THE OFFICE was orderly, even Theo's desk drawers. Beth found nothing out of the ordinary. No envelopes with Canadian stamps, no papers that looked unusual, just livestock sales and purchases, feed bills, bills for supplies to keep a ranch running. There wasn't even anything interesting in the wastebasket.

Flooded with relief, she had already decided there was nothing suspicious here, nothing suspicious about Theo, when her eyes came to rest on the answering machine by the phone. Beginning to feel guilty for her snooping, Beth halfheartedly turned on the "answer play." The first message was from a store in town telling Theo it had a radio part he had ordered. The second message was a man's grave voice, rushed and curt:

"Buffalo, five-thirty Tuesday." Nothing more. It was so unnaturally abrupt that even into the next message Beth was waiting for something else.

She wrinkled her nose and turned off the machine. Buffalo? Could that mean the bar in town by the railroad tracks? The Buffalo Bar was a rough place on Front Street, popular with ranch hands. A sign over the bar boasted that Buffalo Bill Cody once drank there, and it was reputed to have been the site of a fatal knifing once, back before the turn of the century. Beth had never actually been inside the Buffalo Bar, but she'd been curious about it since she was a child. People said it was a bawdy place, and from William F. Cody's day until now it had been a favorite haunt of the local cowboys.

The message had said five-thirty Tuesday. Tomorrow. Theo evidently was expected to heed that summons to be at the Buffalo Bar. It had hardly sounded like a social invitation; it had sounded serious.

There was only one way to find out what was going on, and that was to be there, too. It was probably a crazy thing to do, an act she might be very sorry for later, but Beth was still suffering the prickling needles of a suspicion she was loath to acknowledge. The needles goaded her to take whatever action presented itself, however crazy, however much a long shot. If Theo had anything to do with the theft of those cattle, she had to know it.

It *was* a long shot, yet there was something going on that the caller didn't want to discuss on the answering machine. Possibly there was some connection between Theo's telephone conversation and this summons to a meeting of some sort. In any event, she was going to risk the consequences of trying to find out.

Anyway, she rationalized, it was probably just some kind of cattle-sale deal, the kind Theo was always instigating. So why did she have this awful feeling about it? The wary feeling about Kirk was easier to explain—Kirk was a companion of trouble.

The next day, Tuesday, in the early afternoon Beth rode out to the hills as she had done the day before, hoping Kirk would be there. He wasn't. Her suspicion of him was worsening with every hour. Why had he really come to Prairie Hills Valley? She'd asked herself that a hundred times.

She rode home along the southeast fence, toward Neilson's ranch. It wouldn't be too awkward to stop there; she often did. Tom and Sally Neilson wouldn't think there was anything unusual about her stopping by. In fact, they'd be glad to see her.

Memories of her night with Kirk would not leave Beth. Only two nights had passed, and it seemed like a year. In spite of the fact that Kirk had talked about their not seeing each other for the sake of her reputation, she wanted to see him, to feel his arms around her again. She wanted the chance to make love with him again. Would there ever be another chance, or was that one secret night together all they would ever have?

Sally Neilson was working in the garden. She waved as her neighbor approached. If any men were around, Beth couldn't see them.

"I was just riding by," Beth called. "Thought I'd stop long enough to say hello."

Sally's gray hair was in pigtails. She wore a man's work shirt over her jeans. Pulling off her muddy gloves, she set them on a post. "Come inside, Beth! Let's have some iced tea."

Beth looked at her watch. It was nearly three-thirty. If she was going to get into town to the Buffalo Bar in two hours, she had little time to waste. "Sorry, I can't. I have to run into town soon."

"You've been in the hills?"

"Yes. Everything looks normal up there."

"Isn't it terrible, Beth, the way we have to watch our cattle now? This last theft was the worst yet. And all of them unbranded, they say. Tom's brought most of our horses down from the hill pastures."

Beth groped for a way to bring up Kirk's name, to find out if he was there. "I was at a sale in Sioux Springs last weekend," she began carefully. "Your ranch hand, Kirk Hawthorne, won the champion-bull riding in the rodeo over there. Quite an impressive rider, this guy."

"So I hear," Sally smiled, bending over to pick a dandelion from the carefully cultivated grass in front of her house. "I know he's in trouble with the law, but we—Tom and I—like him. He's always real polite to me and Tom says he's a good worker when he feels like working—which isn't all the time, I understand."

Beth smiled. "You might mention to him that I saw him ride—in the rodeo."

"Surely will. Kirk isn't here now, though. He's over in Sioux Springs again, actually. Hitchhiked over. I was going to drive him but he insisted on hitching instead. He got something in his eye and wanted to have a specialist look at it."

Beth fought to hold down a rush of panic and to keep her voice casual. "I hope it isn't serious. What happened?"

"I'm not sure. He just told us his eye was hurting bad and he wanted to see a doctor. Since there's no eye doctor in Prairie Hills we thought he ought to go up to Sioux Springs to the specialist they got up there. He's been gone since yesterday. He should be back anytime, though. There's plenty of truckers on that road so he shouldn't have much trouble getting a ride."

"You're not, uh, worried, Sally? I mean that he might jump bail up there or something?"

She smiled. "If he does, he does. But I don't think so. Frankly I don't think he'd lie to Tom, though maybe I'm being naive. But that guitar of his is here, and I don't guess he'd leave that behind."

Beth forced a smile. About that much, Sally Neilson was right. Vintage Martin guitars like his were collectors' items. It was a valuable instrument by anybody's standard and particularly valuable to him. Could Kirk really have injured his eye, she wondered, or was he pulling something?

"Tell Tom hello for me," she said. "I have to get on home."

She returned Sally's wave as she started down the tree-shaded lane from their house. Something felt wrong. She hadn't believe his excuse about gambling when he'd missed that first rodeo event. But there was no reason why she shouldn't believe now that he had gone to a doctor. He had injured his eye and she hoped not seriously. Yet something...*something* seemed strange. She just couldn't quite put her finger on what it was.

KIRK HAD BEEN CALLED AWAY early Monday morning, July twenty-first, by a nervous Marty, who insisted he was needed for an important job. There seemed no way to leave the Neilson ranch without inventing an excuse. Tom had not questioned his story about injuring his eye, mostly because Kirk was a good actor, which was the main reason for his success in spy operations like this one. He could convince just about anybody of just about anything. Pain was one of his specialties.

The job Marty had spoken of turned out to be far more grandiose than anything Kirk had expected. This time, when he met a flatbed truck in the middle of the night, he had two dozen calves to move onto an old cattle truck. He knew from the way Marty talked that this was only half of last night's haul. At least this many more animals were being dispersed in the opposite direction by someone else with a second truck.

Luckily, Marty worked with him this time, loading the calves. The two drove together to a tiny sale in Hogg County, where false bills of sale had been provided. This was one of the ways the rustlers avoided discovery—by getting rid of the cattle immediately. No one expected the stolen livestock to turn up that soon.

On Tuesday afternoon after the sale, they drove back to Prairie Springs in Marty's pickup. Kirk was mentally compiling a small list of suspects, but the only way he was going to get any evidence was to follow Marty directly to that evidence. Marty was carrying in his pocket a check from the sale of the calves—a check made out to a phony cattle company. Sooner or later, and probably sooner, Marty had to deliver that check to his boss. With Kirk watching so closely, the meeting would not likely be accomplished without notice; they had to make a slip.

Marty did make a small slip, a very small one, on the drive back from Sioux Springs that day. Before they reached the place at the edge of town where he was to drop Kirk on the road, Marty mentioned that he wasn't going back to work until the following morning. He hinted he was going to stay in town, which might not have been unusual on a Saturday night, but it wasn't Saturday.

This was what Kirk had been waiting for. Whatever Marty planned to do in town tonight, Kirk was going to know about it. Pretending he was looking for a poker game, Kirk asked to be dropped off in town. He didn't intend to let Marty out of his sight.

His thoughts came back to Beth, the way they always did. Thoughts of her had been so vibrant and warm and frequent since Saturday night—their night— that sometimes he had trouble concentrating on his work. By now Beth would have heard he'd been out of town. And she, along with the entire Prairie Hills Valley, would know about the latest cattle thefts, thefts coinciding with his absence. He hoped she wouldn't make any connection. She could be too close to danger if she was to discover anything about this rustling operation—anything at all. Things were about to come to a head; he felt it. He didn't want Beth anywhere near it.

He wished he hadn't had to stand her up for their date in the hills yesterday. She would wonder why. But more than that, he missed her. Maybe he'd have some chance to phone her when he was in town this evening. Unfortunately, that depended on what Marty Schock's secret activities were tonight. A lot of things depended on where Marty was going and whom he was planning to meet.

10

THE STUFFED HEAD of a North American bison hung on the wall of the dimly lit tavern. Its shadow fell on the table in the darkest corner, where Beth sat with her hair tucked under a wide-brimmed hat that helped conceal her face. She had arrived early enough to install herself in the corner, where she sat nervously waiting.

The eyes of the bison bothered her, even though she knew they were made of glass. Slowly turning her mug of untouched beer she stared at the bison thinking how disgusting it was to chop off the head of a magnificent beast and stuff it and hang it in a bar. Barbaric. This one, faded with age, stiffened with dust, obviously had been here for a very long time.

Pictures of Buffalo Bill Cody decorated the dark walls. There were still old men around Prairie Hills who claimed they'd seen William F. Cody here more than once, when they were young boys playing along Front Street and the railroad tracks. Beth had heard stories about this particular tavern all her life, but she'd never thought she would actually set foot in here. Few women ever had.

When a splash of late-afternoon light spilled into the dim room through the opening door, Beth's attention was pulled away from an oversized painting of Buffalo Bill slaying bisons. Others had come in while she sat-waiting, but this time she immediately recognized Theo's tall form. For an instant the light behind him formed a kind of halo shining through his wind-whipped blond hair. She shrank a little lower in her chair, unnoticed.

Theo looked at his watch and made his way to the empty end of the bar, ordered a drink and lit a cigarette. Less than two minutes passed before a cowboy wearing a Stetson hat entered and sat down beside him. Beth recognized the man, although she didn't know him personally. Marty Schock had worked for several of the local ranchers. For some reason, he'd never stayed too long with any of them. This was hardly the person she'd expected her stepbrother to be meeting, although, she conceded, she'd had no idea in the world whom she *had* expected.

The two men drank and talked in hushed tones. It was impossible to catch a single syllable of what they were saying. What good was it to have come here if she couldn't hear any of the conversation, Beth thought with disgust. She should have realized she wouldn't be able to hear anything from the table in the corner. Theo talking to a local cowboy was nothing unusual; no one would think a thing about it. Maybe that was why they'd decided to meet here where no one would look twice at two cowboys talking over a drink in a bar at the end of a working day.

She watched them, frustrated. Finally, taking her drink in her hand, Beth rose and walked slowly toward the bar. Heads turned her way, but she didn't care. Neither Theo nor Marty looked up, though. As she approached them from behind, Theo was saying, "I can't give you any more information on this until I consult with my partner, which won't be until . . ."

Sensing a presence at his back then, he turned around and blinked in disbelief. *"Beth?"*

"Hi! I thought that was you." She took a seat beside him.

"What the devil are you doing here?"

"Just soaking up local color. I was walking by and realized that all my life I'd wanted to see the inside of this place. Besides, I was hot and felt like having a beer after shopping all afternoon." She took a sip, smiling playfully. "I might have known I'd meet somebody I knew. So this is where you hang out, Theodore."

"Now and then." He looked uncomfortable. "Do you know Marty Schock?"

"Not formally." She gave the other man a friendly smile. The smile he returned was forced; the cowhand was not as cool as Theo.

Her stepbrother drew on his cigarette. "You shouldn't be here alone."

"Why not?"

"It's not the best place in town to be. People will get the wrong idea."

"What people? I'm just minding my own business." She looked at him. "Or am I? Am I interrupting your conversation?"

"It wasn't nothing important," Marty said, casting a sideways glance at Theo.

Beth's intuitive senses were finely tuned to their every reaction. Nothing, not the slightest twinge of a lip, could slip by her. Theo was uncomfortable, and it was not for the shame of finding his stepsister in a raunchy tavern. He was uncomfortable because she had seen him here with Marty, she was sure. In hushed tones, with their heads bent over their drinks, they had been discussing something important. There was a difference between casual friends chatting in a bar and men who were talking with a purpose. Even when they tried to conceal it, the difference was obvious to anyone who cared to notice. And Theo was obviously afraid she had noticed.

Beth smiled as if she hadn't a care in the world and began making light conversation. But she was watching them, watching them every second—watching their eyes and their hands. With each passing second, it became harder and harder to pretend casualness, for with each passing second the current of fear in her ran stronger. She hadn't expected to be afraid of Theo, but there was something about him that frightened her, even when he smiled and talked just the way he always did. Marty Schock was not talkative; he was just short of sullen. Both men ordered drinks again.

KIRK HAD REMAINED OUTSIDE the Buffalo Bar after he saw Marty enter. He had this down to a science: it took a man at least ten minutes to drink a beer, and usually fifteen or twenty. If he came in several minutes after Marty and was seen, there could be no proof he was following him. Especially in a place like this, it could be a convincing coincidence.

By the time he entered, the bar was crowded with men just getting off work. When his eyes adjusted to the dim light, Kirk blinked in utter disbelief and drew in his breath. Marty was with Beth and her stepbrother, Theo Lebs!

He stood stunned, just inside the doorway, then slid into a chair at a far table. Watching the three of them deep in conversation at the bar, he felt a wave of sickness wash over him. *Beth?*

It couldn't be! She'd seemed so outraged over the rustling. How could Beth possibly be in cahoots with Marty over anything? Kirk sat in the shadow of the giant bison bull and ground his teeth together. Theo Lebs's presence on a bar stool next to Marty didn't throw him. In fact, in the past two days he'd been thinking a lot about Theo. There seemed to be some correlation between the sales where rustled animals were brought through, with false papers and forged brand inspector's clearances, and the sales where Beth worked. He had begun to think the rustling boss knew Beth's schedule because, of all the stolen livestock that had been taken to auctions, she had found so few. They weren't usually in her territory or at the sales where she worked. It was as if someone knew where she was going to be. Her stepbrother would know. But then, so would several other people.

Nevertheless, Kirk had been thinking about Theo since he learned the people of Prairie Hills knew so little about him or where he came from. His mother had married Beth's father. Otherwise, he wouldn't be here at all. Kirk knew Beth was fond of her stepbrother and that Theo was well liked. But personalities didn't count much with Kirk; he was too experienced as a lawman, having encountered criminals of all kinds.

But Beth couldn't be a friend of Marty Schock's; she just couldn't be! It didn't make sense! Yet here they were in the Buffalo Bar together, drinking—all three of them.

He rose and went to the bar. Not wanting to call attention to any association he had with Beth, he sat down beside Marty, slapping him on the shoulder.

"Never know who you're gonna run into in town," he said while he motioned for the bartender. He smiled a greeting at Theo, who he'd never actually met, and winked at Beth.

She was horrified. The strange looks on the faces of Marty and Theo convinced her that Kirk had come here to meet them. For him to show up here was too much of a coincidence. There had been a scheduled meeting—and the very last person she'd expected at that meeting was Kirk! She felt her mouth going dry as cotton. Kirk didn't seem the least surprised to see her, though. Perhaps he'd been standing back in the crowded bar, watching them.

Marty looked angry. Theo was trying to put up a front of friendliness, but it wasn't convincing. Tension in the air was like electricity. Only Kirk seemed immune to the electric static, Beth noted; he was acting as innocent as a little boy. She could only stare at him—at them all.

Kirk's eye was not bandaged. In fact, it looked as well as it ever did. That eye-injury story must have been a lie, conjured up so he could leave town. And he had left the same day the rustling took place—the same day Theo had made reference to in that phone conversation.

When she managed to find her voice, Beth leaned around Theo's broad shoulders and asked, "How's your eye, Kirk? Sally Neilson told me you had an eye injury."

His hand went at once to his left eye. "I had a splinter in it. It's out now."

"It sounded rather bad."

"It *was* bad. It hurt like hell."

She couldn't judge whether he was telling the truth or not. But there was a doctor in Prairie Hills who surely could have removed a splinter from an eye. Why had he felt he had to go to Sioux Springs to a doctor, unless it was just an excuse? The eye wasn't even bloodshot.

"So," Kirk began after swallowing half a glass of beer, "what was the conversation I interrupted? Don't let me interfere."

"Actually," Beth said in a thin voice, "I was about to leave." Unable to sit there a minute longer, trying to cover her heartache, Beth slid from the bar stool. She was afraid to look at Kirk. Perhaps they all believed she was so naive as to think this meeting had been an accident. In fact, she hoped they believed that was the case, because she wasn't ready to deal with it yet. She couldn't absorb the horror of her own suspicions or accept the fact that those suspicions could be valid. Something was definitely going on here, something the three of them were very anxious she not know about.

It had been bad enough before Kirk showed up. But now she didn't trust herself to control her emotions. She could feel tears of devastating disappointment beginning to form at the back of her eyes, and with desperation she fought down those tears. All she could concentrate on was getting out of there.

She had backed away from them. Theo was suddenly at her side. "I'm leaving too, Beth. Are you on your way home now? I'd like to talk to you."

"Yes, I'm going home."

"I'll be there soon."

"You forgot your newspaper, Theo," Marty said through his teeth.

"Oh, yeah." Theo picked up the newspaper from the bar top.

"That's Marty's paper," Beth said. Theo looked at her so strangely that she was forced to remember she was not supposed to have seen either Theo or Marty enter. She tried to cover the mistake. "I mean, we have the paper at home, Theo. . . ."

He ignored her comment, grunted a farewell to the two men still sitting at the bar and folded the newspaper under his arm before he followed his stepsister outside.

Kirk took a deep swallow of beer before he looked at Marty. He'd had to make a decision whether or not to grab that paper and unfold it right then and there, but this wasn't the way he wanted to do it. Theo would only deny knowledge of that check. Kirk wanted a more open-and-shut case; he wanted a confession. He folded his hand over his glass on the bar top. "We wouldn't want Theo to forget that newspaper, would we, Marty? Not when it's got a fat check stuffed inside."

"I don't know what you're talking about," Marty growled, lighting a cigarette.

"Like hell you don't."

"You better stick to riding bulls, Hawthorne, not to detectivin'."

Kirk smiled a half smile. "So you're a friend of Beth Connor, huh?"

"No, I ain't. Never met her till just now. I seen how you was looking at her, though. If I was you, Hawthorne, I'd watch my step real careful. Theo Lebs ain't a man to cross and if he seen how you was looking at his sister just now, then you got cause to sleep light."

"Yeah? Lebs doesn't look all that dangerous to me."

"I wouldn't count on that if I was you. He's got clout around here, too, and you ain't exactly in a position to make people mad. You got one foot in a jail cell already."

"You're acting awful hostile all of a sudden, Marty. What's the matter? You think I followed you here or something?"

"You're damn right that's what I think."

Kirk motioned to the bartender. "Well. That may or may not be so."

"I came in here for a drink and happened to see Lebs," Marty began. "We got to talking. Then his sister shows up unexpectedly. So go ahead—make a big deal out of it. Who gives a damn?"

"I do. I want to talk to Lebs and I want you to set it up for me. The only way he'll see me is if you set it up."

Marty choked on his drink. He hunched his shoulders, and the beer spilled out when he set down the glass. Kirk pounded his back a time or two.

"What?" Marty howled. "Are you nuts?"

"I said I want to talk to Lebs," Kirk repeated in a flat voice. "Tomorrow. Tell him if he doesn't meet with me, he'll wish he had."

Dark, mean eyes squinted at him. "Is that some kind of a threat?"

"Yeah."

Marty grabbed his sleeve, almost pleading. "What do you want to talk to him about?"

"Money. I want a bigger cut. I want as much as you're getting."

"What the devil makes you think—"

Kirk interrupted, "I've been known to have a big mouth when it comes to trying to plea-bargain myself out of a prison sentence.

"You son-of-a-bitch!"

"Come on, Marty. You knew what kind of a guy you were kicking in with. But I can be bought. You tell Lebs that. I want to talk to him no later than tomorrow."

Marty's eyes were bright with fear. "He ain't gonna be in town tomorrow."

"Are you gonna cross me, cowboy?"

"No, hell, no! But Theo just told me he's going out of town for the day. Denver, probably. He goes there all the time. I'm tell̠ ̠ you the truth!"

"All right. I believe you." He gazed directly into the other man's eyes and squinted. "As soon as he gets back, he and I are gonna talk about money. Have you got that?"

"Okay! Okay."

Kirk, feeling sick inside rather than victorious, threw some money on the bar and left abruptly. His mind was on Beth. The man he was after was her stepbrother, damn it! All he had on Theo so far was circumstantial, though. And Marty was more hindrance than help because he was too afraid of Lebs to ever cross him. Kirk needed proof. He expected to get it when he confronted Theo Lebs in person.

He walked out into the shadows of twilight. The sky was pinking in the west, over the low buildings of the little town. A train whistle sounded in the distance, a lonely, mournful sound to match his mood.

Beth herself had reported discovering some of the altered brands, he remembered from the sheriff's reports he'd read. When they'd met that first time, by the windmill, she was certain he was a horse thief. That was real. Her fury over her friends' severe financial losses because of the rustling was sincere. He was trained to know people and he was convinced he knew Beth. The more Kirk thought about it, the more convinced he was that she had nothing to do with her stepbrother's crimes. She certainly hadn't known that newspaper was a secret exchange.

How much, he wondered, *did* she know about Theo? Could she have any suspicion that her stepbrother was head of the entire rustling operation? He strongly doubted she knew. But if she did, Kirk asked himself, would she protect him?

Whether it looked good to anyone or not, he had to talk to Beth, and the sooner the better. She could be in the middle of something she didn't know anything about—something that could get her in very serious trouble. If Theo was away all day tomorrow, that would make it easier to reach Beth. What he would say to her Kirk didn't know. He only knew he felt afraid for her and he had to see her.

BETH HAD NEVER FELT so alone in her life, or so afraid. Theo had delivered a convincing story about why he had met Marty Schock at the Buffalo Bar. He'd said it had to do with the rodeo committee, which he was volunteering for in the coming year. He'd been sweet and casual, just the way he always was. By the time he'd finished, Beth had almost begun to question her sanity in suspecting him of any wrongdoing at all.

Yet something inside her knew he was lying. His left eye had been squinting. Theo and Marty and Kirk had not been at the Buffalo Bar as casual friends. It was too coincidental, and there had been far too much friction going on for that to be true. They'd been there because it had been prearranged. The business was not the rodeo committee and she knew it. It was something far more sinister.

She wanted desperately to talk to Kirk, but the idea was ridiculous. Beth had known all along he was a criminal; she'd known this and ignored it, pretended it wasn't true. What the devil could she expect if she fell in love with a man like that? Lila had tried to warn her.

Lila. Oh, poor Lila! Beth sat in the bay window of her silent room with tears in her eyes and thought, *I can't even talk to Lila! I can't talk to anybody!* The suspicions about Theo, and about Kirk, were only suspicions and would have to be kept inside her. But protection wasn't what Theo and Kirk deserved; they deserved to be turned in to the sheriff. How could she, though, when she loved them both? Even if she knew for sure—how could she? Beth was well aware that she had no proof for suspecting either of them. Mostly it was intuition. Certainly she couldn't tell Lila what she thought Theo was up to, even if she was sure she was right. And the possibility remained strong that she was wrong. Sitting in the dark, Beth prayed she was wrong. She thought of Kirk's tender hands in the night and his lips on hers and his deep voice singing a special song he'd written for her, and she prayed that she was wrong. In one day, one plain summer day with a sunrise like any other day, her life had become a nightmare.

ON TOM NEILSON'S SORREL, Kirk rode to the Circle C Ranch the following day, just as the late afternoon was turning to evening, when he knew Beth would be home from work. He wasn't eager to think about what sort of reception he was going to get from her stepmother, because Beth had said enough for him to realize the woman vehemently disapproved of her seeing him. Not that he could blame her. But he didn't want to deal with that issue tonight or with Lila Connor. He just wanted to talk to Beth, without any interference from anybody.

The air was cool because the afternoon had been dark and rainy. Now, at five o'clock, it was still raining. Minutes ago it had begun to pour. Riding up to the ranch, Kirk saw that the barn door stood open and there was a light on inside. He dismounted and walked through the open door, leading his horse into shelter from the rain.

The air in the barn was warm and smelled of sweet, fresh hay. Kirk saw no one. He shook rain from his hat, hung it on the saddle horn and threw his plastic rain jacket aside. After wrapping the reins of his horse around a railing near the entrance, he walked toward the back of the spacious building, past a row of open stalls.

He didn't know how he knew, but he was sure Beth was in there. And he was right. She was kneeling in the hay in a corner stall playing with four tiny kittens. Because of the sound of the rain on the roof, she hadn't heard his steps in the soft straw. He watched her for a time, thinking about the softness of her. Softness of her hair, flowing over her shoulders. Softness of her touch as she handled the tiny, delicate animals. Softness of her body, the sweetest memory he had ever known. Softness of her laugh when one of the kittens rolled sideways onto another.

She didn't see him until he was kneeling beside her, reaching for one of the kittens himself.

"Kirk! You startled me."

"I'm sorry. I didn't mean to."

"Your jeans are wet," she said, and then after an uncomfortable pause, "Why are . . . you here?"

Her voice sounded strange. She didn't seem to want to look at him. Kirk sat down beside her in the straw. "I want to talk to you, Beth. It's important."

"I really don't think . . . I don't want to know, Kirk. I don't want to know anything. I don't think we have anything to talk about."

"Where's Theo?"

"I should think you'd know that better than I."

He frowned and looked at her quizzically. "Why would I know where Theo is?"

Kirk rubbed the back of his neck. He'd never seen Beth act cold. Something had changed. It had changed in the Buffalo Bar, when she'd left so abruptly, hardly having spoken to him, except to ask about his eye. He'd been too dumbfounded just seeing her there to give much thought to her strange behavior. Now, watching her, sensing a coldness that had never been there before, he was beginning to understand. She thought *he* had been involved in that meeting with Theo and Marty! Of course! What else could she think? He was, after all, an established thief already. It wouldn't be hard to believe he was continuing his criminal activities. And he *had* come into the bar only minutes after Marty.

Beth's reaction was probably the answer to one question that had been bothering him, about whether she suspected Theo. Apparently she did. Kirk wondered how long she had suspected him, if she'd been covering for him, and whether she would continue to cover for him. How much did she know?

He sat back in the straw, allowing a kitten to crawl over his legs. "There's no way I could know where your stepbrother is. I'd never talked to him in my life before yesterday, at the Buffalo."

Beth looked at him, her eyes full of hurt and confusion. His heart went out to her.

"Why do you want to know where he is, then?" she asked.

The answer to that question was becoming clearer to Kirk by the minute, and he hated it. He was genuinely afraid for Beth's safety! There was something about Marty's attitude yesterday.... Kirk had correctly read the anger directed at him, but there had been more. He realized Marty must have been telling the truth when he'd said Beth's presence there was a surprise. Kirk doubted it had been accidental, her being in that place; there had to be some explanation for it. But whatever the reason, Marty hadn't liked her being there. And probably neither had Theo. Beth had stumbled onto something and put herself in more danger than she knew.

Kirk was the only one who could protect her. But he couldn't tell her so!

"Did you have something to talk to Theo about?" she asked abruptly when he didn't answer her first question.

"Where is he?"

"Denver. He flew up this morning and said he'd be back in the late afternoon."

"He's not back yet?"

She glared at him. "Why?"

Kirk sighed deeply. He picked up a white-and-gray kitten. "Beth, you have to trust me. We've been...we've been very close, and . . . and that's important to me. I care about you. You've got to trust me."

For a moment she looked as though she would have liked to hit him. "Who—" her voice broke "—who can trust *anyone*?"

"You can. Believe me. Please trust me."

Her eyes, dull and sad, looked into his; she simply stared for what seemed to him a very long time. Her gaze was so filled with confusion that her eyes seemed to change colors, from dark to light and then to dark again. Finally she asked, for the second time since they'd met, "Who . . . are . . . you?"

"I'm . . . not what you think I am."

"I don't even know what I think you are, except—"

"Except a thief and a drifter. I'm neither."

She sat back in the hay and blinked. In the silence, one of the kittens mewed. She noticed Kirk's fists were clenched. Whatever he was telling her, he didn't want to tell her; that much was clear. What *was* he telling her? Beth felt as if she couldn't breathe. Her heart had started pounding.

"My arrest here," he said in a voice barely above a whisper, "was phony. Sheriff Arnold hired me to pose as a criminal."

"Hired you?" Her voice was flat, disbelieving. "Why would he do that?"

He rubbed his neck again. "I came to Prairie Hills to try to infiltrate the rustling ring. My arrest was part of the setup. I couldn't tell you. I couldn't tell anybody without jeopardizing my chances of doing what I came to do."

"What? Kirk, what did you say?"

"You heard me right. I didn't want to lie to you, but I had no choice."

"You're not . . . not a thief . . . not waiting trial . . . ?"

"No. I'm not a thief."

While she stared at him all the color left her cheeks.

"Why are you telling me this now?"

"Believe me, I didn't want to yet. But you have to know that I'm . . . here. That you don't have to feel frightened or alone. I'm here, and I'll protect you."

His voice seemed to be coming through a tunnel, like an echo, real and unreal at the same time. Believable and unbelievable. "Pro-protect me from what?"

"From anything...or anybody...who threatens you."

His words were washing over her like a cool ocean wave, and the heat that had been inside her seemed to be steaming from the sudden relief. Only now was Beth allowing herself to admit how frightened she'd been since last night. Theo had come into the living room after they'd got back from town, and he hadn't been the same person. He'd been pleasant, joking even, but not the same. She'd tried to pretend otherwise. But he hadn't been himself, and the person he was had frightened her. She was a threat to Theo, and he knew it. And he didn't like it.

"Kirk, is this true?" she asked in a breath, not a voice.

He nodded. Moving close to her, he kissed her temple tenderly.

"Did you . . . infiltrate the rustling ring?"

"Yes. But I couldn't find out who the big boss was. He kept his identity very guarded."

"Do you know yet who he is?"

"Yes."

Beth didn't want to look at Kirk. Instead she watched his hands—large hands holding the soft kitten. The tiny animal had settled down sleepily in his palm, and Kirk held it as if he held kittens every day of his life. In a shaky, fear-filled voice she asked, "Is it Theo?"

He swallowed, feeling her pain. "Yes, I'm afraid it is."

"How long have you known?"

"Only since yesterday at the Buffalo Bar. I was following Marty." He looked up. "How long have *you* known?"

"I . . . I haven't been able to face it. I really can't deal with it, Kirk. but I . . . when I heard about the rustling that took place on the twenty-first, I knew I had to face up to my suspicions, much as I hated to. I had overheard a peculiar phone conversation of Theo's referring to that day. The conversation didn't make any sense, but I knew something was terribly wrong. Then I picked up a message on his private answering machine about a five-thirty meeting at the Buffalo. It was such an odd message, so abrupt, that I was suspicious of it, so I went to the Buffalo before five-thirty to see who Theo was meeting. All this time, I intuitively knew something dreadful was going on. Little things, you know. Like Theo's bank account in Canada. I didn't find out anything the least bit incriminating at the Buffalo, though, except that he met Marty and, I thought, you."

"And I thought Marty was meeting you both. That gave me some very bad moments, Beth."

"You thought I . . . ?"

"I didn't think it for long. I just . . . knew you too well to believe it."

"Oh, Lord!" she said. "Oh, Kirk! What's going to happen?"

"I have to get proof Theo is the guy I want."

"H-how?"

"It won't be hard as long as he believes I'm a thief who was hired to work from him. I'm going to set up a meeting with him as soon as I can. Tonight, I hope. I'm sorry, Beth. I'm sorry it turned out to be someone you care about."

"Haven't you . . . haven't you taken an awful chance telling me all this, Kirk? I mean, I could warn my brother. . . ."

"Yes, you could. But I don't think you will. If I'm wrong about you, then I've lost all faith in my perception of human nature."

Beth could only stare at Kirk's hands. The kitten's white fur formed silky little frills around his fingers.

He continued, "In fact, I don't think you should be around him at all now that he thinks you could be a threat to him. He could be dangerous. I just don't like you being here now, Beth."

"He'd never . . . harm me." She didn't sound too sure.

"I've been around a little, honey. I've learned about people. Don't trust Theo if he's cornered; he has a hell of a lot to lose if he's found out. I've seen what desperate people are capable of. That's why I felt I had to tell you who I am. So you'd know someone is looking out for you."

She gazed at him incredulously. It was still sinking in. "You're a spy?"

He grinned. "I guess you could call it that."

Beth closed her eyes. An incredible sensation of lightness had been lifting her and was lifting her still. Not only wasn't Kirk a rustler, he wasn't a thief of any kind! He wasn't awaiting a jail sentence. He was a spy.

Since yesterday her thoughts, her very world, had become so dark. Thoughts of Theo still—so dark. But the darkness was tempered now by an incredible lightness that engulfed her. The lightness was Kirk! She lay back in the straw, sighing a tremendous sigh, letting the lightness support her.

Kirk's voice, so deep and wonderfully familiar in the darkness behind closed eyes, echoed through the silence of the old barn.

"Why are you laughing, Beth?"

"I can't help it. Kirk, I really believed you were an incredibly charming, aimless, gorgeous, worthless, lawbreaking bum!"

He moved closer, touching her cheek lightly. "Did you honestly believe that?"

She opened her eyes and looked up at him, at his blue eyes. The laughter in her own eyes faded to pensiveness—to somber cognition. *No,* she thought. *No, I didn't honestly believe it because it never fit.* This man was an excellent actor and teller of tales and he had fooled a lot of men. But a woman who loved him saw other things—the gentle things, the good things.... *No.* Her soaring heart thundered. *I never did believe it.*

She raised her arms to him, and he came nearer to kiss her. "I didn't believe you were a bum, Kirk. I thought I did, but reflecting on my feelings now, I knew better."

"I counted on that," he said.

"Kirk...I'm scared. You said you were going to meet with Theo. What are you going to do?"

"Get him to admit he's head of this whole damn rustling operation by threatening blackmail."

"It sounds dangerous."

He kissed her forehead lightly. "Don't worry about me. You're the one who—"

Suddenly a new fright seared Beth's consciousness like a bolt of lightning. She sat up so abruptly she hit his chin with her head. "Kirk! Oh, Lord, I just remembered something!"

11

KIRK RUBBED his throbbing jaw. "What is it, Beth?"

"Theo has a partner!"

His light eyes squinted. "What makes you think so?"

"I just remembered! He said so! When I walked up behind Theo and Marty at the bar, I heard him saying he had to check with his partner about something." She closed her eyes, trying to hear the remarks in the ears of her memory. "Yes, that was it. He said he had to check with his partner before he could let Marty know about something and that he wasn't sure when he'd be talking to that partner. I can't recall the words exactly, but that was the gist of it. I'm sure I'm not mistaken about the partner. I heard it distinctly. Kirk, I'm sorry I hurt you just now...."

He was still rubbing his chin but was too absorbed in thought to react to her remark about banging his chin with her head. "You say he's in Denver today?"

"Well, maybe I only assumed it was Denver because he goes there often. Do you think his partner could be in Denver?"

"His partner could be anywhere. Damn." Now it was the back of his neck he rubbed.

"He told Lila he was coming back this afternoon. He left early this morning, but he isn't back yet. At least, I didn't hear his truck come in."

Kirk swore under his breath. "I don't like this, Beth. I don't like you being here. I've got to...." His voice trailed away.

Once more she asked, "What are you going to do?"

"I can't confront him here," he said. "Theo wouldn't talk to me here, anyway. I'll have Marty set up a meeting place for tonight."

"Will he do that?"

"I can persuade him."

"I don't like the sound of that, Kirk!"

He smiled. "You worry too much."

She closed her eyes. "Only moments ago you said desperate men can be dangerous. You said—"

"I can take care of myself."

"But, Kirk, there's someone else—the partner! Someone you don't know about."

"Yeah. It might be very interesting to see whether or not Theo shows up alone, after Marty tells him about the threats I've been making."

Fear gnawed at her insides. "How can you set yourself up like that? This is absolutely—it's a nightmare! Kirk, how did you get mixed up in this in the first place? Where did you—"

The sound of a truck engine in the drive stopped her. Her eyes grew wide and frightened. "It's Theo!"

"I don't want him to find me here. It'll ruin my strategy. Do you think he'll come into the barn?"

"Probably not, but I can't be sure, with the light on in here. I'll go on out and meet him. After Theo and I are in the house you can leave without being seen."

Before he had a chance to answer, Beth was on her feet and heading for the door. She turned once to let him know that it was, indeed, Theo's truck out there, switched off the light and closed the door behind her. Kirk's horse gave a small whinny, too low to be heard.

Dusk lingered; the rain had become only a drizzle. Somewhere up there in the clouds would be a full moon, but it had not yet risen. Wet prairie grass darkened the cuffs of her jeans.

The dog, James, had already met Theo's truck. Beth walked to the front porch and, leaning against the railing, waited for him.

Dressed in jeans and a denim jacket, Theo ascended the steps two at a time. "Hi, Beth."

"Hi." She fought to keep her voice casual. "Did you know we have a new litter of four kittens in the barn? Gertrude's again. They must be two weeks old already. She's kept them hidden until now."

"I hope they're all good mousers." Theo slipped his arm around her shoulders as they walked together toward the front door of the house.

At his affectionate gesture, a gesture so familiar, her heart sank into aching. The ache of grief.

She asked, "Where've you been today?"

"I flew up to Denver to check on that registered Hereford bull I told you about last week."

He had mentioned a bull he was considering buying. "Did you see the bull?"

"No. We were supposed to fly out to the ranch by helicopter, but something went wrong with the damn thing. The trip was a total waste of time. I'll try next week, but I have a feeling the bull is overpriced."

Inside, he headed for the dining room. "I'm for a drink, Beth. Want one?"

"No, thanks. I'm going upstairs to have a bath. I'll see you at dinner."

She passed Lila on the stairs. "Oh, Beth, dear. I was just taking some fresh flowers up to your room. My yellow roses are blooming profusely in the side garden."

Her stepmother kept fresh flowers in the house all summer long. Beth had become used to it and loved it. The yellow and pink roses from the east garden were so fragrant their delicate aroma filled a room.

"Thank you, Lila," she said, forcing a smile. Her head was beginning to ache badly. Facing Theo had been more difficult than she had imagined—trying to act as though everything was the way it had always been. Now the presence of Lila started the ache in her head to throbbing. Poor Lila! Theo was her only offspring, and she adored him. This shock was going to just about kill her.

"Are you coming down for a cocktail before dinner, dear?"

"Not for a while, Lila. I've got a headache and I just want to soak in a hot tub for a while."

I can't do this, she thought. *I can't sit through dinner with them as if nothing is wrong, as if the whole world hasn't changed.* She remembered the countless dialogues they'd had at the dinner table about the rustling. She remembered when they themselves had lost livestock. Could Theo have staged the theft of his own cattle to put suspicion off himself? Possibly, since everyone else in the valley had been robbed. But her palomino? Oh, surely he wouldn't have stolen Party Girl when he knew how much she loved that horse!

Alone in her room, Beth felt the full burden of the hurt like a heavy weight upon her. She had believed in Theo. She genuinely liked him. How could he possibly be the person behind all this rustling? If only this whole thing turned out to be a colossal misunderstanding or a bad dream. She hoped, without really hoping.

But Kirk was not a dream. He was real. And for all the gentleness she had seen in him when they were together, she was aware of quite another side to the man she loved. He could be rough, even violent, given cause; she knew it. It was a rough man's world in which he lived. And Theo might well give him cause, if Kirk goaded him. Damn, Kirk *intended* to goad him. It was part of his bizarre "strategy."

Who the devil was Kirk? she wondered. Where had he come from? She had started to ask him just before Theo came home. He had volunteered nothing, absolutely nothing, about himself. Not a word about his private life. All she knew was that he was a spy—a man pretending to be someone he was not. He could be from anywhere, be anyone. He might even have a wife, for all she knew.

He was so good at pretending. Beth wondered in the solitude of her room how much of his feelings had been pretense. Had he withheld any personal information about himself because he was so preoccupied with what was happening today and with concern for her safety? Or was there some other reason—something he was deliberately holding back?

While she was soaking in the tub the phone rang several times. Each time she felt a pang of fright, remembering Kirk's self-assured claim that he could induce Marty Schock to set up a meeting with Theo tonight.

She swallowed three aspirins for her headache and forced herself to get dressed. It would take all the self-discipline she had to get herself down to dinner tonight, but she intended to make herself do it. Theo was already on guard about her. Any unusual behavior on her part might convince him he had something to worry about. No matter how difficult it was, she had to act as if nothing was wrong.

She dressed in a pale-blue summer skirt, a white blouse and white sandals and tied her hair back with a blue ribbon. At seven o'clock she went downstairs. They always ate at seven, but usually Beth was there early to help with the meal. Tonight the last thing she could think about was food, either preparing it or eating it.

It seemed too quiet in the dining room. The table was set as usual with fresh flowers in the center and place settings for three. Lila came out of the kitchen with a water pitcher and proceeded to pour water in only two of the glasses.

"Theo won't be here for dinner," Lila said. "He got a phone call about a meeting of some sort. The rodeo committee or something. He didn't say."

Alternating emotions of relief and fear whirled through Beth's aching head: relief that she wouldn't have to face Theo at dinner; fear for the confrontation she knew was coming between Theo and Kirk. Someone could get hurt in that confrontation.

Her heart went out to the woman who was happily setting the table for dinner. Beth wished there was something she could say, some way she could forewarn Lila that her whole world was about to come crashing down on her. There was just no way to say it. Beth clung desperately to a thin, frayed thread of hope that she was wrong—that Kirk was wrong. The idea of Theo's being behind the rustling was too horrible to face, especially here in their pleasant dining room with his mother and the meal for three that Lila had prepared.

Beth went to the kitchen to help bring the dishes to the table. Lila was happily chatting about her latest project—drying fresh flowers in sand in the oven, to make into floral arrangements in picture frames.

When they were seated at the table, Beth said, "The meat loaf smells wonderful, Lila. I love your cooking, but I still think you should consider getting a cook. It really isn't necessary for you to have to make all the meals."

"Good heavens, cooking is a pleasure for me, and we only have two meals a day here. Breakfast is nothing, and cooking dinner gives every day just that much more purpose. A cook would just get in the way, and anyway, how would we find someone who can cook as well as I can?"

"You definitely have a point there."

Lila smiled. "You're not eating much tonight, Beth."

"Just not very hungry, I guess."

"You have a lot on your mind."

Beth nodded. She felt extremely awkward, miserable. This was like a bad dream. And yet, in the midst of the nightmare was a recurring whirl of joy—joy that the man she had fallen in love with was not the criminal she'd believed him to be. She wasn't sure who Kirk *was*, but she knew he wasn't a thief destined for prison. If anything was going to separate them from this point on, at least it wouldn't be that. For the first time it seemed as if their love had a chance, some chance, anyway—if Kirk really did care for her. And if he was free. The possibility sent her heart soaring, even through the bleak clouds of despair she felt because of Theo and now sympathy for Lila.

Lila's smile had faded. There seemed to be something on her mind. "I saw a horse ride up earlier," she said finally, while she buttered a hot roll. "From the window the rider looked like Kirk Hawthorne. He went right on into the barn as if he owned the place."

"It was raining. He came in to protect the horse—and Tom's saddle."

"What did he want? As if I couldn't guess. He's in hot pursuit of you. Anyone could see that."

"He just wanted to talk to me."

Lila set down her fork, worry lines forming on her forehead. "Have you been seeing this man, Beth?"

Beth looked at her plate. She didn't want to lie about it. The whole evening—the whole day—seemed like nothing but a great series of lies, one after another. Beth felt like a hypocrite even sitting here pretending she didn't know anything was going on this minute between Kirk and Theo.

"You *have* been seeing him! Beth, dear, how could you? You've always been so levelheaded and sensible. Surely you're not letting this man fast-talk you into believing he cares for you or anything as ridiculous as that."

Beth was put immediately on the defensive. "You mean ridiculous that a man could care for me?"

"Please! You know what I mean. You know exactly. He'll try to get all he can out of you, and marriage if there's any way he can convince you how wonderful he is. He's a criminal, Beth. And I don't know why on earth he's running loose all over the place when he ought to be in jail. And I . . ." Lila paused and leaned forward, frowning. A hard line had formed around her usually soft lips. "I don't like that look that came into your eyes when I mentioned Kirk Hawthorne's name. You're eyes almost lit up! Surely, Beth, dear, surely you can't be thinking of having anything more to do with a man like that!"

It was not a complete surprise to Beth that she couldn't hide her feelings from Lila. Her thoughts were so full of Kirk, her heart was so full of him, that it couldn't help but show, especially tonight, after what he had just told her about himself. She could deny it all night long and not fool Lila, Beth knew.

The need to defend the man she loved was becoming stronger with every passing moment as Lila's barrage of insults continued. Finally Beth blurted, "It's not what you think!"

"What isn't?"

"Kirk isn't. He's not . . . what you think he is."

The older woman looked stricken. "Oh, dear heaven, you're defending him. He *has* influenced you, hasn't he?"

"I like him, if that's what you mean. But you needn't get so upset about it, Lila. There's really no reason to be so upset."

"No *reason*?" Lila had paled.

Beth's heart went out to her. Her stepmother was acting out of concern for her, Beth knew. She wanted to protect her from hurt. Perhaps she also feared that if Beth were to marry someone like Kirk Hawthorne, he would push Theo out as manager of the ranch. But mostly, Lila wanted to protect her, and Beth didn't resent this. She herself had known drifters and seen one of her friends taken in by one. Lila was right about them. She wished she could put Lila's mind at ease, but she didn't dare say too much. Still, Kirk's real identity would be known very soon, perhaps even before the night was out. And by then Lila would have a lot more to worry about than Beth's relationship with a stranger. That very stranger was about to accuse her son of rustling.

"Kirk isn't what everyone thinks he is," she said defensively.

Lila blinked. She seemed to grab these words as one might grab a rope to keep from falling. "What do you mean, Beth?"

"Just that you're wrong about him."

"I don't understand."

"I can't . . . explain. I just want you to please not be so uptight about it, okay? I'm not going to be taken in by a . . . drifter."

Lila sat back, sucking in her breath. Beth noticed her hands were shaking. Her voice was soft but very strained. "Beth, I've known you for many years now. I know you well. That's why it has never made sense that you could fall for a common criminal. You just aren't that kind of woman. This man . . . tell me about him."

Lila's trembling hands confused Beth. This unusual pressing about Kirk was out of character for Lila, who was sensitive to Beth's reactions and usually dropped a subject if Beth pulled back. She seemed to be pressing harder and harder, so hard that Beth was becoming nervous.

Under the scrutiny of Lila's dark eyes, Beth got the sinking feeling that talking about Kirk tonight might have been a mistake. Lila was acting strangely—over-reacting to the few comments about Kirk, almost as though she didn't *want* to be encouraged about Kirk Hawthorne's moral fiber.

"Well?" Lila was asking, still wringing her hands in the same unusual way. "Tell me about this man who sneaks into our barn at night."

"There's nothing to tell, Lila. And he didn't sneak."

"Where does he come from?"

"I don't know for sure. Montana, I think."

"If he isn't who everybody thinks he is, then who is he?"

"I don't know."

Lila stared at her, her eyes squinting, her brow wrinkled as if she was deep in thought. Suddenly she pushed her chair back from the table. "Excuse me a moment, Beth. I'm going to the bathroom. I'll be right back."

The sinking feeling was still lingering. Lila's behavior just wasn't quite right; she hadn't been her usual self since Beth's comment about Kirk. And she had left the room so swiftly without looking back.

Beth rose and went out into the wide hallway. The library door was shut and the light was on inside. Pausing outside that door, Beth could hear Lila's muffled voice, but she couldn't tell what she was saying. Lila had obviously been so anxious to get to a telephone she'd lied about going to the bathroom in the middle of dinner. Something was wrong, and it had to have something to do with their conversation about Kirk.

Beth moved away from the closed door and slipped into the living room. As carefully as possible she lifted the extension from the receiver, hoping the tiny click wouldn't be heard.

At once she realized it wouldn't be. There was a lot of noise coming from the other end, noise like a radio, and through the noise was Theo's voice saying, "Are you sure about this?"

"Sure enough to feel I had to warn you," Lila answered in a low voice. "I just didn't like the sound of it. You're not alone with him, are you?"

"Marty's here."

"But is Kirk? Is he there yet?"

It seemed he was there; Theo was forming his answers very carefully. He paused, and during that pause Beth could hear the radio, which wasn't an ordinary radio. It sounded like a C.B. with a man's scratchy voice, and what she could hear of it made no sense. She caught the words "log head," "gandy dancers" and "yard goat." And "brass pounder."

Theo answered hesitantly, "Yeah. Don't worry, I'm hearing you real plain." His voice was grinding with anger.

He hung up. Reeling with shock, Beth replaced the receiver. Her head was swimming. Theo's partner was Lila! It was the last thing on earth she'd expected.

She ran her fingers through her hair, her heart thundering. What had she done? Shot off her mouth enough for Lila to get jittery about the meeting. Theo was warned now, and Kirk was in danger. Very possibly he was in grave danger.

Lila was Theo's partner! Beth said it over and over to try to make it real, but it was impossible to believe. In seconds Lila would be back in the dining room. Beth was desperately trying to figure out what to do. There was no way to warn Kirk now, because she had no idea where the meeting was. Lila knew; she had known all along. But that was no help. Shaking and pale, Beth slipped back into the dining room and sat down again.

But Lila didn't return. Instead she called from the hallway, "Beth, I'm not feeling very well. I'm going to my room to lie down. Please don't worry about the dishes, dear. I'll take care of them later. I may want some dessert later, but not now. I'm sorry to be rude, but I feel I must lie down."

"Of course, Lila," Beth answered, greatly relieved. She couldn't have talked to Lila now; it would have been impossible. Beth heard the woman's footsteps disappear in the hallway and her bedroom door close. If Lila were to leave the house Beth would see her car, but she knew she wouldn't leave. She'd warned her son; it was all she could do.

Beth paced the room, more desperate than she'd ever felt in her life. Kirk was in danger because his cover was as good as blown—thanks to her—and there was nothing she could do about it. Tears of frustration formed in her eyes. She pounded her fist into her palm repeatedly. "Where are they?" she kept muttering aloud. "Where are they?"

IN A SMALL TRAIN DEPOT three miles from the edge of town the air virtually crackled with a surge of electricity as Theo put down the phone. All eyes in the room were on him. The silence was like the pause just before a lit fuse hits the dynamite. The radio squawked and cracked, but no one heard it. They heard only Theo's silent fury.

Kirk tensed like a cat ready to spring, but not before his prey moved. Theo was flanked by two large men, Marty on one side and Shroeder, the station telegrapher, on the other. During the past ten minutes of heated negotiation, he had already sized up Shroeder as a formidable enemy. The telegrapher was a man in his early fifties, large and burly, with a badly scarred hand and a built-in scowl on his face. He wore his loyalty to Theo like a badge of honor; there would be no cracking that loyalty, and Kirk knew it. Nor Marty's, either. Kirk had gotten himself into a situation more hazardous than he'd intended. He had thought Marty might be at this conference, but he hadn't expected anyone else. He figured Theo's partner would prefer to keep out of sight. Shroeder was not that partner, he'd decided. Shroeder was on duty here at the depot.

He wished he had a gun. But Marty had fleeced him, as he thought he would; he'd never have gotten inside with a gun even if he'd brought one. And had they found a gun on him, his bargaining position would have been badly jeopardized. Theo would not make concessions to a man hotheaded enough to carry a weapon.

Yet Theo was armed. Kirk's trained eye could see the outline of a small handgun under his shirt. And Shroeder very likely had a handgun in his desk drawer; telegraphers often did because they worked long hours alone at night. Shroeder was not near his desk now; he was standing a few feet from his boss.

Theo's eyes had become fiery while he was talking on the phone. Now he turned to Kirk. "It seems," he said in a grave voice, "we may have a problem."

Kirk met the challenge of his enemy's angry eyes by returning the steady stare.

Marty took a step toward Kirk, then moved back again uncertainly. "Whatsa matter, Theo?"

"Mr. Hawthorne here isn't who he says he is. We have a spy among us."

Kirk smiled. "That sounds fancy as hell, Theo. Who were you talking to to come up with a story like that?"

"A reliable source." He was glaring. His hand moved to his shirt, over the weapon inside.

Shroeder took a step toward the desk. His eyes, too, were fixed on Kirk. "Spy?" he repeated incredulously. "*Spy*? You better say who you are, mister!"

Kirk held his ground, not moving an inch. "The name's Bond. James Bond."

"You bastard!" Marty howled. "You think this is some damn joke?"

Kirk smiled viciously. "It's Theo with the sense of humor. Oh, hell, yes, I'm a spy. Don't I look like a spy? What'd I walk into here? A ring of lunatics?"

The radio's almost constant squawking was being ignored by Shroeder, until suddenly, in this tense moment, he became alert. The scratchy voice was saying, "... bad ass at the big hole..." The message was evidently for Shroeder. He swore under his breath and moved toward the radio, grabbing for his tablet to write down some incoming numbers.

"Never mind that!" Theo demanded.

"There may be an emergency at a crossing," the telegrapher protested. "Some idiot went across the tracks in a car and the train had to hit the air—"

"Was there a collision?"

"No... but if they have to walk the train..."

Theo was furious. His hand was on the buttons of his shirt, over the hidden gun. Kirk watched those hands like a wary cat watching a mouse.

"Knock off that lingo and speak English!" Theo growled. His ears were red. "If there's no accident what are you supposed to do about it?"

"Somebody got the car license...." Shroeder's faded eyes were pleading. "Look, if I don't—"

"All right, take the damn message, then." He drew the gun from his shirt and aimed it at Kirk's heart. "For somebody who ain't who he says he is, Hawthorne, you know way too much."

"Are you gonna add murder to your resumé?" Kirk asked, his eyes on the weapon that was pointed at him.

"We're isolated out here. Nobody knows we're here."

"That's right," Marty confirmed. "I brung him and we wasn't followed or nothing. There ain't nobody knows we're here except—" His gray eyes darted toward the telephone.

"Don't worry about the phone call," Theo said. "My partner knows where we are, but nobody else does."

At these words, the telegrapher looked up from the radio, his face registering shock. Kirk didn't miss it. Whoever that had been on the telephone—the man Theo called his partner—Shroeder knew. He must have recognized the voice. And the partner's identity surprised him.

"You don't expect me to let you walk out of here, do you?" Theo was saying to Kirk.

Kirk turned to him. "I don't think you're a murderer."

"You think wrong. I'm up to my neck already. I'm not gonna let anything go wrong now, because of you. Was this a setup, Hawthorne? Some kind of big setup?"

It was too late to try to argue his way out of it, Kirk knew. Whatever was said on the phone had convinced Theo he was a spy. It was strange, that call, because no one knew except the sheriff and . . . A knot formed in the pit of his stomach. *Beth was the only one who knew! No*, he told himself with desperation. *It couldn't be!* Why had Shroeder been surprised by the voice of Theo's partner? Possibly because the voice belonged to a woman?

There wasn't time to speculate on it now. Time was running out. Kirk felt the heat of Theo's temper and vibrations of desperation from the other two men.

"I'm a gambling man," Theo was saying. "If I wasn't, I never would have got into this chancy business in the first place. I been careful not to slip up anywhere, but it looks like we've been tricked by some damn wandering rodeo cowboy. Who are you working for, Hawthorne?"

"For myself. For whoever offers me the most money."

The other man smiled. "You could be telling the truth, but this time I can't take the chance of believing you. If you disappear, mister, nobody is going to know from where. They won't find you. And they won't link me to you."

"I wouldn't count on that."

Kirk knew it was useless to try to stall any longer. Theo was desperate enough to kill him. Theo *intended* to kill him. Moving like an uncoiling snake, Kirk made a sideways lunge toward the man, knocking him to the floor. A gunshot rang through the still air and echoed against the walls of the tiny train station.

THAT RADIO! It was no ordinary radio broadcast because it had been loaded with words that didn't make sense. Beth sat on a chair in the dining room, head in her hands, and tried to think. To remember. They were crazy words, yet vaguely familiar from somewhere deep in her past. Hog head—that was one of the phrases she'd heard. Hog head. Yard goat. Was it a C.B.? It seemed like more of a dispatch of some kind. . . .

"Gandy dancers," she said aloud. "Where have I *heard* that? Yard goat. Hog head. Brass pounder."

She sat up straight, her eyes opening wide. "Brass pounder!" That was it! She remembered now. Years ago she and her father had been in the old train station to send a telegraph message, and she'd sat while he talked with the telegrapher and listened to the messages sent on the radio. Train and telegraph dispatches! She had heard that same crazy expression then: gandy dancers! And when she'd asked, the telegrapher had told her it was their term for section men, repair men. Messages had come over the wire constantly but the telegrapher had paid attention only to occasional ones—the ones coded especially to him. The other messages had been for different towns along the rail line.

Beth sucked in her breath. There were railroad radios in all the surrounding towns, but Theo hadn't been gone long enough to have driven very far. There was only one such radio anywhere near Prairie Hills—the one at the railroad depot!

It was a small station, not well used because only one train a day actually stopped at Prairie Hills. It sat on the outskirts of town between a dirt road and the railroad tracks. In the old days there had been buildings around it, but they had long since been torn down. Only the old station house remained out there, isolated.

Beth's heart was thundering. There was no question in her mind that this was where they were right now! Theo's voice had literally trembled with anger on the phone. Lila's warning had made him furious. And Marty Schock was out there, too, so there were at least two men against one. Beth's blood ran cold with fear.

Beth looked up at the clock on the wall. Two minutes had already gone by since Theo had hung up the phone. Time was precious and time was moving. She had to do something to warn Kirk—she had to! Beth ran up the stairs two at a time and grabbed her purse and truck keys from a table in her bedroom.

She was out on the county road before she began thinking clearly. What did she think she was going to do when she got to the station house? It had never occurred to her to grab a gun. Beth closed her eyes. No, the very idea of carrying a gun was unthinkable!

But the danger was very real. Kirk was in deep trouble, and the kind of help he needed right now wasn't the kind she could give him. It was too late for warnings. What Kirk needed was not her but the sheriff!

She stepped on the gas. The nine miles to town seemed like a hundred. When she pulled up in front of the county jail, Ollie Arnold, who must have been working late, was just coming out of the front door.

She stopped in a no-parking area and ran to him, out of breath.

"Ollie, we've got to get out to the railroad depot! Kirk is in trouble out there!"

He twisted his cigar and stared at her. His bulbous nose wrinkled. "What the devil, Beth?"

"Please! We need to hurry! He's with Theo!"

This didn't bring any immediate reaction. Obviously Kirk hadn't alerted the sheriff to this showdown meeting or even to his suspicions about Theo. He must have been waiting for proof and hadn't believed he was taking enough risk tonight to ask Ollie for any backup.

"Slow down there, Beth! I don't know what you—"

She was yanking on his shirtsleeve. "Kirk Hawthorne didn't tell you he had set up a meeting with Theo tonight?"

"No."

"He told me, though, Ollie. He told me he's been working with you to find out who's behind the rustling. He suspects Theo. But Theo knows something's wrong and Kirk doesn't know Theo knows! Oh, Ollie, just hurry! They're at the train station and Kirk is in danger! We have to get out there!"

The sheriff emitted a wild oath and rushed toward his car. "You'd better stay here."

"No! No, I won't!" Before he could protest any further she was in the passenger seat of his car.

He screeched out of the drive and picked up the radio to call for a backup car. The siren went on.

The ride was a nightmare for Beth. Red and blue lights whirling around them like something from a horror film. The frantic voices booming over the police radio. Ollie's voice answering, directing his deputies to the depot just outside of town. Echoes of the awful phone call: Lila's voice warning Theo; Theo's fury; that radio in the background . . . Thank heavens for that telegraph radio, she thought. If only it wasn't too late. She kept looking at her watch, but inside the police car it was too dark to see it.

The streets were wet from the earlier rain, making the lights shine even more eerily. But the sky was clearing. The moon had risen full in the sky. Clouds moved over it, swinging on a high wind. But nearer to the earth the air was calm and fresh– washed from the summer rain. Except for the high, blowing clouds making occasional shadows over the yellow globe, the moon was visible and big and casting its light over the valley.

Beth was frantically trying to calculate. The best time she'd ever made into town going the speed limit was fourteen minutes. Tonight she was sure she'd made it in ten. Add three minutes that it took her to get out of the house, another one or two at the sheriff's office and two or three now to get to the station. Sixteen or seventeen minutes since Theo had hung up the phone. Were they going to be in time, or had something terrible happened in those minutes?

Sheriff Arnold pulled up to the depot. "Stay back, Beth. Stay in the car." He pulled out his gun and opened the door.

Beth's heart was pounding in her throat as she watched him approach the building. She opened the car door and got out but, heeding his warning, stayed well back in the shadows. She didn't want her presence to make things worse than they were already. This whole thing was her fault for talking to Lila about Kirk!

A shot rang out from inside the station, followed a few seconds later by another. Beth's heart nearly stopped. Her eyes closed; she couldn't move. Fear immobilized her. The sheriff kicked at the door with his gun drawn. The door came open easily, and his large form disappeared from the doorway. There was no sound from inside.

"Kirk!" Beth cried aloud. Her body suddenly came to life, and the same fear that had frozen her seconds before now pushed her forward, stumbling, toward the depot. "Kirk!"

Behind her the second sheriff's car was arriving in a blaze of red and blue flashing lights, siren blaring. It came to a stop and three deputies, all brandishing guns, leaped out. One of them yelled at her to get back as they came up from behind, rushing for the building.

On legs that would barely hold her, Beth reached the doorway. Kirk was standing in the center of the room, holding a gun in his hand. Theo was backed against the wall, Marty and a strange man against another. No one appeared to be hurt. Relief washed over her like a flood. Kirk was all right, and so was Theo!

"How the devil did you get the gun?" Ollie Arnold was asking Kirk.

"I ducked and jumped him and managed to deflect his arm—a trick I learned from kung-fu lessons years ago. Don't look at me like that, Ollie! I know it wasn't a smart move, but I had nothing to lose by trying it. I was about to get shot anyway. The gun fired, but luckily Lebs lost his hold on it when I hit him, and I managed to grab it."

One of the deputies picked up a second gun from the floor beside the desk. "Whose weapon is this?" he asked, holding it in front of him.

The sheriff walked over to take it from the other man. He studied the gun for several seconds, then scowled at Shroeder. "It belongs to the telegrapher. He tried to take it out of his desk just as I was coming in the door. Kirk fired a warning shot past Shroeder's head and made him drop it on the floor."

The deputy stared at Kirk. "What the hell? You managed to disarm two men?"

Kirk brushed back his hair from his eyes. "I managed to get the gun. Persuasion is a matter of whoever has his finger on the trigger at the time." He looked at the sheriff, puzzled. "How did you know where I was?"

"Beth told me."

The knot in Kirk's stomach tightened. "Beth?"

Trembling, she came forward from the shadows of the doorway. "Kirk, thank heavens you're all right! I heard Lila phoning to warn Theo."

"She picked up the phone," the sheriff explained, taking over because Beth's voice was shaking so, "and heard the railroad telegraph radio in the background and figured out from there where you were. I swear she must have driven a hundred miles an hour over that river road."

Kirk scratched his head. "Lila? Theo's phone call was from his mother?"

"Yes," Beth answered. "Theo's partner is Lila. I didn't know until I heard her on the phone. I could hardly... hardly believe it...."

"Lila," Kirk repeated, and shook his head, frowning. "Damn..."

"I panicked, knowing I had to find a way to warn you," Beth said weakly. "But it looks like you had things under control here." She looked at her stepbrother and then quickly away because she couldn't face Theo. This moment she felt she didn't want to look at him ever again; it would hurt too much. But she had to look at him—had to talk to him. She had to know!

Grasping Kirk's arm for support, she turned to her stepbrother. Her voice cracked. "Theo, *why*? Why would you and Lila do this?"

He glared at her through the coldest eyes she had ever seen. "Because my mother was cheated. She deserved at least half interest in the Circle C. Did you really think I'd be content managing somebody else's land all my life? Lila and I were cheated."

"But you even stole from *me*, Theo. My horse . . ."

"Hell, if you'd really cared about Lila or me you'd have given us interest in the ranch. We're the ones who did all the work, kept it going for you. . . ."

Kirk took a step toward him. "You bastard! Beth gave you free use of her grazing land and her cut hay—*and* her house!"

Beth shook her head in disbelief. "I can't understand, Theo, I just can't. . . ."

He grinned sourly. "What's so hard to understand? My mother and I needed enough money to buy our own ranch and we sure weren't going to get it working for you."

The sheriff's deputy warned Theo, "Anything you say can be used against you, Lebs. I already told you that. Just don't forget it."

Theo jerked away from him. "What the hell difference does it make? Hawthorne came here for proof and he's got it. I'm not pretending he hasn't."

Beth's knees were shaking. She sat down on the desk chair and watched in a blur while the deputies went about the business of clearing out the building. The radio kept squawking, but no one paid any attention to it. On the way to the depot Beth had told Ollie what she knew about Theo and Lila. There was nothing more to say, nothing more to do. Except cry.

She buried her face in her arms on the desk, shutting out the sight of her stepbrother being led away in handcuffs, wishing she could as easily shut out the sounds around her. The radio was quiet for several moments, and then started yammering again. Kirk was all right. Thank God. But her foolishness in trusting Lila had nearly got him killed.

Everything in her life had changed in one thin hour. Everything. Theo and Lila would not be part of the Circle C anymore, not part of her life anymore. They would have to stand trial. She shuddered and couldn't bear to think about it. Beth felt ashamed, betrayed, angry. How could they have done this—to her, to all the others? How could they have lived in her house and lied to her all these months while they were stealing from her and from their neighbors?

Betrayal was a heavy weight for her to bear, but another was worse. She felt overcome with a feeling of loneliness and sadness greater than any she had ever known. The disbelief had gone. Sadness had taken its place.

When a hand came down on her shoulder, Beth raised her head. Kirk's silver-blue eyes were gazing down at her.

"Beth?" he whispered. "Are you okay?"

She blinked up at him. "Kirk. How did you do it?"

"Do what?"

"Get the better of three men? And two guns?"

"I was lucky. But let's not talk about it now. It's over."

"You act as though it was nothing! As though you do this sort of thing all the time. I nearly get you killed and you don't want to talk about it!"

"It wasn't your fault."

"Of course it was! You asked for my confidence and I said something to Lila about her being wrong about you. I didn't say very much, though. I didn't have to. She was so alert to my every word, every emotion, she . . . she . . ."

"It wasn't your fault," he repeated.

When a tear spilled from her eye, he circled his arm around her and pulled her up and toward him, into his chest, and held her. He whispered, "You can't blame yourself for not suspecting Lila—for trusting someone so close to you, someone you care about. I didn't suspect her, either. Not once."

"But, Kirk . . ."

"Shh. It's over, Beth. It's over sooner than I thought it would be, and for that, I'm grateful."

She sniffed and looked past his shoulder to assure herself the room was empty. They were alone now. The police cars were pulling away, their sirens shrieking through the silence of the little town. Theo was gone, and with him a part of her life. All these years she'd believed he genuinely liked her. She'd believed they both did, when all the while they were so obsessed with jealous resentment they'd resorted to crime to get away from the Circle C and to get even because they believed she and her father had cheated them. All these months . . .

Kirk's arms felt solid and steady when everything else in her world had crumbled away. She allowed herself the luxury of his arms and his warmth while he held her.

"Kirk, I don't see how you can be so calm after your life was threatened, after all that's just happened."

"Honey, it's part of my job."

She looked up at him and asked, for the third time since they had met, "Who are you? Tell me who you are."

"I didn't realize I hadn't told you. I live in Tumblecreek, Montana, where I work part-time as a deputy sheriff. A few years ago I managed to get myself hired into a gang of rustlers by pretending to be a thief. A national group of cattlemen alerted Sheriff Arnold to that fact, and I found myself with a job down here in Prairie Hills. What I didn't figure on—" he ran his hands affectionately over her shoulders "—what I didn't figure on was meeting you."

"I thought you were a professional rodeo rider."

"I was once. That was several years ago."

Beth sighed shakily. "What else are you? Are you—"

"Come on," he interrupted. "Let's get out of this place, Beth. That radio is driving me nuts. Let's just . . . walk."

He took her hand. She followed in silence. The night was fresh and cool from the earlier rain. Fragrance of prairie grass and wildflowers rose out of the dampness. The dirt road led away from the railroad tracks, and as they followed it, the full moon lent enough light for them to see by. Because gravel from the road kept getting into her sandals, Beth walked slowly, falling behind, dragging on his arm.

Kirk finally stopped. "This has been hard on you, Beth. Damn. I know how much you care for your stepbrother and your stepmother."

She nodded. There was nothing to say. His arm came around her shoulders as they started to walk again, slowly, in the direction of the town. "We don't have to walk," he said. "Ollie is going to send a car back for us. The cars were a little crowded. I thought you'd prefer to wait . . . with me."

"Yes." Her voice was flat, stunned. She clutched his arm for something solid to lean on. "It's going to be a terrible scandal, just awful. To think the woman my father married...the man who lived in my house at my invitation and managed the ranch...my adopted family..." She shuddered. "Oh, Kirk, it's going to be horrible to have to face people! Just...horrible...." Her voice, breaking, faded away.

She found herself being urged gently toward him again, into his arms. He whispered, "I'm sorry, honey. I wish I could make this night go away."

His lips brushed over hers, lightly at first; then his kiss deepened. She closed her eyes and allowed herself to be swept into the kiss—into the escape of his kiss— and the moonlight became warm on her skin.

His husky whisper came again as he held her against him. "I wish I could kiss away the pain."

She thought, *it's over. His job is over.* What—or whom—did he have to return to now? He had abruptly changed the subject minutes ago in the depot when she'd tried to ask him more about himself, his life. "Tell me . . ." she breathed, almost afraid to know. "Tell me . . . who . . . you are. . . ."

Kirk fell into a strange silence. For her, dread grew in that silence. He'd answered her question and she just kept asking. No, Beth thought, he knew he hadn't answered. He knew exactly what she meant. His silence frightened her.

A train whistle sounded in the distance, such a lonely, mournful sound, trailing out of the darkness. And then came Kirk's voice—husky, the way it had sounded when he was making love to her. "I'm a man who loves you, Beth."

She gazed up at him, at his face in moonlight. Her heart nearly stopped beating.

He bent to kiss her again. She felt so small in his arms, so strangely helpless. His kiss rendered her more helpless still.

From the echoes of his kiss she heard his deep, throaty voice say, "I'm the man you're going to marry. Don't you know that yet?"

Beth's eyes shot open. She saw the sky bathed in moonlight, saw swaying shadows of trees along the roadside, shadows moving with the rhythm of the balmy night as if they were a symphony. The shadows danced over them like a canopy of song.

She sought her voice, not trusting it to come. "Did you just say *marry*?"

"Honey, are you so surprised? I thought you knew I loved you."

"I . . . hoped. Oh, how I hoped! But I didn't know anything about you. I didn't even know . . ." She sighed deeply. "Oh, never mind all that! Kirk I . . . I love you!

Oh, yes, you are the man I'm going to marry! You really are!"

He laughed. "I haven't had a chance to tell you much about me."

"You're an ex-rodeo champion. And a deputy sheriff."

"I'm a rancher, too. I own half a ranch near Tumblecreek. I don't work full-time as a deputy because of the ranch. Could you be happy living in Montana?"

"I could be happy anywhere, with you. Anywhere you are . . . I want to be." Her head was swimming with a giddiness that seemed to cause a fuzzy glow to settle over everything. The words came out of her as if the world hadn't turned on its axis in the past minute, with Kirk's declaration of love, his proposal of marriage. There was no chance to absorb it.

"Montana is far away. You told me once how you hated to leave your ranch."

"Kirk, I'll go with you. You're more important to me than anything else." She gazed up at his doubt-filled eyes. "It's better if I leave this valley, anyway." Her voice shook as she said it. *Leave this valley.* She had to now, because of what had happened here. Now, faced with disgrace, she wanted to leave.

Kirk smoothed back her hair gently. "I'll take you away from here as soon as I can."

"To your ranch?" She grasped his arm tightly. "Kirk we'll have . . . we'll have two ranches!"

"Yeah, I guess we will."

"Who runs your ranch when you're working as a deputy?"

"My partner, who is also my brother."

"You have a brother?"

"I have two brothers," he smiled. "Both in Tumble-creek. Both ranchers. And my mother lives near there, too, in town. So you see, darling, you may have lost one family tonight, but you've gained another. My family is going to welcome you and love you just like I do."

"Your family..." she repeated in a small, half-believing voice. "Only a few minutes ago in the depot, I was feeling so alone. And now... now like magic, I have a family?"

"Yes. You have a family." His lips brushed her forehead. "I wish we could leave here tonight, right now. But we can't. My job's not finished. It won't be for several days yet. I don't want you to have to be alone at the ranch, honey. I'll stay with you. When will you marry me? Tonight?"

She looked up at him, stunned. "We'll have a wedding, won't we?"

He looked surprised, as though he hadn't thought of it. "A wedding? Yeah... of course."

"Here in Prairie Hills?"

"Whatever you want. I think the bride should choose." He smiled again and straightened. "Hot damn, what a beautiful bride you'll be! I'm the luckiest man alive!"

Above them cottonwood leaves clicked melodically, trembling in the night breeze. A thousand leaves touching, singing. An owl hooted from somewhere in the leafy branches. The magic of the moment was broken by approaching headlights.

Sheriff Ollie Arnold, grinning broadly, pulled up alongside them. "I hope you two wasn't planning to walk all the way back to town."

"We trusted you to come back for us." Kirk opened the door of the back seat for Beth and got in beside her.

"This is one helluva night," Arnold said. "In all my years of sheriffing I ain't never had to arrest a woman I've tipped my hat to many a time, nor a man I've called my friend." He looked at his passengers through the rearview mirror. "Beth, I'm real sorry. This ain't gonna be easy for you. This town is gonna be angry."

"I know, Ollie. I'm trying to brace myself."

He lit a cigar. "What I can't figure, Kirk, is how come you told Beth who you were if you suspected Theo Lebs?"

"I had my reasons, sheriff."

Ollie scratched his head, cigar between his fingers. "Hell, and when other folks learn who you really are, that's gonna be still another jolt around here." He grinned. "I hope you're braced good, Beth. There's gonna be a helluva shock to this town come morning."

13

THE SCANDAL rocked the valley. The arrests of the widow and stepson of Charles Connor and the charges of rustling against them set off public outrage the likes of which Beth had never seen. It was far worse than she had anticipated, although she realized she should have expected it. Hers was one of the most highly respected families of the town, a family of pioneers. Her father, Charles, and his father before him had been admired and respected and had no enemies that Beth ever knew of. Now Beth couldn't walk down the street in Prairie Hills without feeling the stares and hearing the whispers.

It was she who had established Theo Lebs here as comanager of her ranch, she who had trusted him, and because of her, so had the people of Prairie Hills valley. She accepted the burden of blame and felt none toward them. How could she blame the people of the town for talking of nothing else? They had a reason to be angry.

And so did she. Theo and Lila had betrayed her. They had put her through this embarrassment, ruined her reputation and that of her father, who had married Lila. Beth had believed they were family; they had stripped her of just about everything she believed in.

The county jail was small and there were no proper visiting facilities. When she had gathered the fortitude to see Lila, Beth was led through a set of locked doors to the far wing. The prisoner sat in a chair, reading by the light of the window. Shadows of the bars on her face were dark, unnatural. When she saw Beth, an expression of surprise came to her eyes, but it quickly turned to blank indifference. Beth stood outside the cell fidgeting with the strap of her leather handbag, and it was a long time before either woman spoke.

"I didn't expect to see you here," Lila said thinly.

"I needed to talk to you." Beth looked around the aging jail. "Why are you here, Lila? Why aren't you out on bail?"

"Just where would I go? To your house?" She waved an arm in dismissal of the subject. "It isn't safe for me out there, or for Theo. People are acting like a lynch mob. And all thanks to you and that . . . that rodeo cowboy or whatever he is."

A wave of anger rushed through Beth. "I hope you're not blaming somebody else for what's happened. You and Theo must have known the risks you were taking. I just don't understand, Lila. I don't think I'll ever understand. Why on earth did you do it?"

"I believe Theo told you why."

Beth shifted from one foot to the other. "I had no idea you were so unhappy at the ranch. You were always so sweet, so cheerful. I can't believe you let Theo talk you into being part of a serious crime like this."

The older woman looked up and smiled. "My dear, it wasn't Theo's idea; it was mine. I resented it every time you walked into that house. It was my house."

"Your . . . ? I grew up in that house, Lila! So did my father."

She seemed not to have heard. "I deserved a home of my own. Theo, too. We just wanted enough money to buy our own ranch. Theo's smart, you know. All he needed was a chance and he could have made it big. Your father could have given us that chance if he hadn't cheated us out of the ranch. I always assumed I'd have at least half. I wanted that for Theo. I knew he was smart enough to work out a scheme for getting a lot of money. There's money in stolen cattle; I knew that. I don't know why you had to interfere and ruin everything for us, Beth. We never did you any harm."

You stole my horse for starters, Beth thought, but she didn't say it. Her stomach was churning; she was becoming physically ill from this unbelievable encounter. Lila was unreachable; there was no use even trying to break through the wall of resentment. She decided not to visit Theo. There was nothing left to say.

"We never did you any harm," Lila repeated accusingly.

Backing away, Beth only stared and muttered, "You've hurt me now, Lila," while she motioned to the guard at the hallway door that she wanted to leave.

The sheriff wasn't in that afternoon, so there was nothing to detain Beth, no excuse to linger inside the building before she descended the outside stairs. If she was lucky no one would see her. No harm, she thought, steaming with anger. No harm, when they'd only threatened, if not taken, everything she believed in. And even more: Lila and Theo had taken one of her dreams away from her—a dream she'd had since she was a little girl—of a fairy-book wedding in the big, beautiful church where she had been baptized. She couldn't have that wedding now, not in the midst of all this furor, the whispers and the stares. She was disgraced. And the dream was gone.

Her anger was not gone. How dare Theo and Lila take even her wedding away from her!

"HOW DARE THEY!" she raged to her closest friends, Kay Trimble and Janet Mataush, as she sat in Kay's living room having coffee. "When I think of the times we all sat in this very room when we were growing up and talked about our weddings, and now I'm really going to get married to the most fabulous guy on the planet and I want it to be so wonderful, for us both—a day to remember forever. I've dreamed . . . remember how we dreamed? I always thought it would be so perfect. . . . Oh, I'm so damn mad!"

Janet pounded a fist on the couch cushion. "You shouldn't have to give all that up!"

"I know. But the whole town has exploded with the fury. Everywhere I go, there's nothing else on anybody's lips. They sort of hush up when I come around. Then I can hear it starting again, with stares at my back. I hate it."

"Well, don't give in to it," Kay said, offering around a small plate of cookies. "You don't have to give in to it."

"Well, no, I don't. I could plan my wedding just as if it never happened. But everyone would be thoroughly shocked if I did anything that brazen. No one would come."

Janet grinned. "I'd come."

"You'd have to come. You'd be in it."

"Oh, I would, wouldn't I? I'd be your bridesmaid! Kay would be your maid of honor, of course, and Billie Jean would be a bridesmaid.... What would we wear, Beth? Oh, beautiful gowns! What color?"

Beth's eyes lit up. "The gowns? Oh, you'd wear lavender! I always said my bridesmaids would wear the color of lilacs. And, Kay, you'd be in lavender, too, but a darker shade. And I'd have my mother's lace gown and white roses—" Beth stopped herself abruptly. Tears sprang to her eyes. "Oh! Damn! It would have been...so nice...."

Kay set down her coffee cup. "We're going to do it, Beth! Never mind everybody else! We're going to have your wedding just as if this thing had never happened. We'll plan everything. It'll be as beautiful as you ever dreamed!"

Beth stared at her best friend, just sat and stared.

Janet chimed in at once. "Yes! Of course we will, Beth! We'll plan it anyway!"

She felt like crying. "No one would come."

"Who cares? We'll be there—and your groom will be there. Marylou will play the organ—she'll love it. Your best and true friends will be there, Beth. Oh, please, say yes!"

"Yes! Oh, yes! Let's do it! It will be a small and private affair, but—"

"But beautiful!" Janet raved. "Absolutely beautiful. Lilac gowns and white roses and...what's your mother's dress like?"

"It has a train six feet long! I think it may have to be taken in a little."

"We have a million things to do. First, to reserve the church. What day, Beth? We have a million things to do. How long do we have?"

"Oh, dear." She tried to think. "Kirk will be finished with his work here by next week . . . unfortunately he has to be here for the formal arraignment. I guess we have only about a week."

"We'll do it! With Billie Jean and Marylou and Trish—the six of us! If we start right now, this minute, we can do it!"

"There won't be the problem of getting invitations printed or catering food," Beth said. "We can just plan cake and champagne for about a dozen people. Let's keep it quiet, okay? Not tell anybody else about this? Because people are talking enough as it is."

Kay nodded in agreement. "Sure. Private weddings are the best, anyhow. It'll just be very . . . exclusive. That's the word: exclusive!"

Janet rose. "Let's drive to Denver tomorrow morning and pick out our dresses. We can plan everything on the way there and on the way back. Shall we?"

Beth smiled, feeling a hundred percent better than she had felt an hour ago. "What will I ever do without you two when I leave Prairie Hills?"

Kay sobered. "I wish you weren't leaving. Montana is so far. What's going to happen with the Circle C when you leave?"

"I asked Kirk if he thought his brother would be interested in coming down here to manage it while Kirk works the ranch up there. He talked to his brother yesterday, and I'm sure we're going to be able to work something out. Everything . . . kept in the family. . . ."

"Kirk has a brother?" Kay asked.

Beth nodded. "If his brother comes down here, which I think he will, then I won't be truly leaving! Because we'll be coming back to Prairie Hills often. Kirk and I talked about it. He understands how much this ranch means to me. We'll sort of live in two places. He'll probably quit his job as deputy to ranch full-time. I hope so."

"What about your job?"

Beth shrugged. "Maybe they'll need another brand inspector. If not, there'll be more than enough work for me to do . . . at home. I'm as good a ranch hand as the next guy."

"But you'll be coming back here often. That's the main thing!" Janet jumped up to hug her.

"Yeah!" Kay chimed. "But, whoa! Back up there a tiny bit. What about Kirk's brother? Is he married?"

Beth smiled. "He has two brothers. One of them isn't married."

"The one who might come here?"

"Yes. He's younger than Kirk."

"Oh, my God! What if he looks like Kirk!"

"Maybe he does."

Kay fell back into the soft cushions. "Now, there's *my* dream! I get to meet him first because I spoke up first. Don't forget who's first in line here!"

"Without even asking how old he is?"

"Who cares!"

Beth sighed, thinking for the thousandth time how lucky she was. How could anybody else look like Kirk? How could anybody else *be* like him? As exciting, as gentle, as strong, as beautiful? She mused, "Sometimes I'm sure I'm only dreaming when I think about Kirk. Especially when I'm trying to believe he really wants to marry me."

Janet gave her a playful shove. "Stay conscious, Beth! We've got a hell of a lot to do and just a few days to do it in!"

"Kirk Hawthorne has a brother," Kay repeated. "Is that ever the most interesting news I've heard in my life."

Beth met Janet's eyes and both women dissolved in laughter. It was like a hundred other get-togethers in this room. Nothing had really changed.

Yet everything had changed, because the local sheriff had asked a Montana deputy sheriff to come to Prairie Hills.

BUSY DAYS ROLLED TOGETHER like a snowball down a mountain, gathering momentum. They were days of joy and sorrow but mostly joy because Kirk's love was there. Kirk's incredible strength was there. The hurt could reach her, but not as deeply, not as painfully as it would have if he hadn't been stationed between her and the rest of the world, understanding her loss, bolstering her gathering strength.

He supported her plans for the wedding, even though she felt he probably didn't understand why everything had to be so elaborate for such a little gathering. If it bothered him, he never said so. He didn't even balk when she asked him to be fitted for a rented tuxedo.

By mutual agreement, he didn't stay at the Circle C. People were talking enough about them as it was. Beth stayed in town with Kay, and in a frenzy of excitement, she tried to isolate herself from the eyes and ears of the town and enjoy the anticipation of her wedding and becoming Kirk Hawthorne's wife.

THEY DRESSED in a side wing of the church. Their bouquets filled the room with the fragrance of roses. Their petticoats rustled. Lilac silk of the bridesmaids' dresses, deep lavender trimmed in ivory for the maid of honor, white lace for the bride. Laughter and giggles and glasses of champagne. Organ music from the big, open sanctuary of the church.

Beth was trembling with excitement, knowing she was not as nervous as she would have been had the church been filled with people, as in her dream. But still, the church was beautiful, with candles and flowers, bright sun streaming through the stained-glass windows. It would be a long trip down the aisle past empty rows toward the handful of her very closest friends in the first two pews. But Kirk would be there, waiting. Nothing else in the world could change the wonder of that. Kirk, standing beside his brother. The best surprise of her wedding-eve dinner was learning Kirk's younger brother had come to stand up with him at his wedding.

Her attendants fussed and hurried her. The wedding march was about to begin. Beth followed them out into the vestibule, where Kay's father was waiting to take the bride on his arm. As the doors were flung open, she gasped and stepped backward as if to get her balance. The church was filled to capacity!

The bridesmaids paused and turned surprised eyes back to Beth. Kay let out a little shriek. She turned around. "Beth! Beth, look at this! No invitations and this church is full!"

The wedding march had begun once and now began again, in earnest this time. Janet started down the aisle.

As Beth walked, white roses trembling in her hands, the audience stood, smiling. Here were faces from her earliest memories, faces of classmates, faces of her father's friends, her mother's friends—her friends. The people of Prairie Hills. It seemed as if the whole town were here! Their faces began to blur through a haze of tears.

She blinked to clear her eyes, leaning more heavily than she intended on the arm of Kay's father.

Kirk was standing up there behind an array of flowers, looking far more handsome in his tuxedo than Beth had imagined he would. Her thoughts ran crazily. She thought of the first time she had ever seen him— lying naked in the sun—turning silver-blue eyes on her in anger.

These were the same blue eyes, looking now upon his bride. And giddily, crazily, she thought, *if it weren't for Theo and Lila being thieves, I would not have met him. He wouldn't have come here, and I would not have met him!*

She felt the vibrations of love around her, behind the smiling faces, as she walked slowly to the cadence of the wedding march. Every step took her nearer the future, with glimpses of her future—Kirk's eyes in sunshine...Kirk coming home to a warm fire and to her....

During the short ceremony he took hold of her arm and stood very close to her, supporting her with his strength and his warmth. But for all his strength, his voice broke once with emotion.

When the bride and groom started back down the aisle, the uninvited guests stood as a body and applauded.

"These people..." Kirk said in the midst of cheers. "I thought...."

"So did I." She smiled. "But I was wrong."

The reception line was a marathon of hugs and afterward, in the Crystal Ball Room of the Prairie Hotel, there was a three-tiered wedding cake and champagne and even the local band for dancing. It was a lavish party arranged by Kay's parents and other friends as a wedding present.

Old Mrs. Tucker had too much to drink and began to sing. Dr. Osterhout began throwing olive seeds. Kay danced four dances with Kirk's brother, Greg, and set tongues to wagging. And the school principal, Mr. Malone, on his sixth glass of champagne, winked at Mrs. Fenderhoff, the president of the P.T.A. Everything was as it was supposed to be.

And Beth had never felt so loved.

THE UNPAVED ROAD was rough, but Beth hardly felt the jars to her spine. The air was cooler here, but the skies were as blue as the skies of western Nebraska—and as big.

"Mother lives in town, but she insisted on my bringing her out to your house early this morning," Chuck Hawthorne said. "She wanted to get the house cleaned for you, so everything would be spiffy. You know Mother."

Kirk smiled and tightened his arm around Beth's shoulders. "This is it, honey. We're home."

Kirk's older brother, who had met them at the airport, steered his truck into a long drive, edged with trees. A large house came into view. It was an old house, recently remodeled. The lawns were very green, and the barn and outbuildings were spread out and well kept. Kirk helped his bride down from the high truck. She paused, breathless, and looked around her. To the east, as far as she could see, was open country with grazing cattle, and in the distance was a windmill. It was beautiful. The most beautiful place she'd ever seen.

She smiled up at her husband, too awed for the moment to speak. From the porch a gray-haired woman was waving.

Kirk waved back and took Beth's hand. He smiled. "There'll be pie and cookies in there, I'll bet. And neighbors later on—to welcome you. Are you happy?"

Her voice was choked with emotion. "Yes . . . I'm happy."

"Welcome home, Mrs. Hawthorne," Kirk said, sweeping his bride into his arms. "I'm not putting you down again until we're inside our own house, and maybe not even then. Maybe not ever."

Harlequin Temptation

COMING NEXT MONTH

#177 TEST OF TIME Jayne Ann Krentz

New bride Katy was thrilled by her husband's ardor and by the prospect of sharing a lifetime with him. Too soon she discovered the real reason Garrett had married her....

#178 WIT AND WISDOM Shirley Larson

For a man whose lovemaking was more than eloquent, Joel was tongue-tied when it came to those three little words Alison longed to hear. It was high time to persuade him that words could speak as loudly as actions....

#179 ONE OF THE FAMILY Kristine Rolofson

Allie had just popped into the post office to pick up a few letters—and ended up with one angry male! But even though her rambunctious kids had accidentally destroyed his bicycle, Michael quickly saw the advantages to being stranded....

#180 BEFORE AND AFTER Mary Jo Territo

Verna Myers found the willpower to shed some pounds, and chose a spa to do the job. Then robust fellow guest Mel Hopkins made an unintentionally grand entrance into her life. And Verna suspected food would not be her only temptation....